"If you think I did this only for Tim, you're wrong. It was a way to get you out of the house so we could talk. You wouldn't have come if we hadn't brought Tim, would you?"

"No, I confess, I wouldn't have. You're not like anyone I've ever met, Hank. You have an overwhelming personality," she said, lowering her gaze, "and you know you're much more sophisticated than I."

Hank chuckled, shaking his head at the frank statement. "And you are a very honest girl. Do you realize how rare that is?"

"I'm not being honest today."

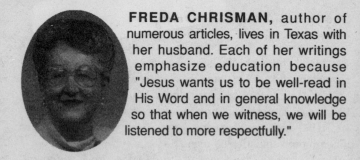

FREDA CHRISMAN, author of numerous articles, lives in Texas with her husband. Each of her writings emphasize education because "Jesus wants us to be well-read in His Word and in general knowledge so that when we witness, we will be listened to more respectfully."

Books by Freda Chrisman

HEARTSONG PRESENTS
HP233—Faith Came Late

At the Golden Gate

Freda Chrisman

Heartsong Presents

To my daughter, Keri; my mentor, B. K.; Sally; Andrea; and Chris, the man who believes in me.

A note from the author:
I love to hear from my readers! You may correspond with me by writing:

Freda Chrisman
Author Relations
PO Box 719
Uhrichsville, OH 44683

ISBN 1-58660-068-0

AT THE GOLDEN GATE

All Scripture quotations are taken from the King James Version of the Bible.

All of the characters and events in this book are fictitious. Any resemblance to actual persons, living or dead, or to actual events is purely coincidental.

Cover illustration by Ron Hall.

PRINTED IN THE U.S.A.

one

Emily Anderson had heard of people dying in the desert. But until she'd endured hours of its savagery, she could not imagine such heat. Patting her wet forehead with her handkerchief, she watched clumps of sagebrush, stands of cacti, and red and white Burma Shave signs slip past the window of the lumbering bus. In the distance, bare sculpted hills of red rock and clay stood sentinel in an otherwise barren landscape.

She returned the hankie to her new purse, a twenty-second-birthday gift from a teacher friend, and relaxed against the worn seat back. *Should we have stayed in Brewster?* she wondered. Would California be a repeat of their last summer in Kansas?

No. Nothing could be worse than their desperate life in the dust bowl, as it was now called. This was their second chance, and whether their fortunes improved or not, there was no going back.

Except for the love of friends, the Andersons' ties to Kansas were severed. They'd sold their family home and furnishings to fund their escape to the Golden State. Although she'd taught first grade for the past year, Emily had graduated from teacher's college only two weeks ago and now felt certain she'd find a job in San Francisco. Not all teachers had degrees, but at present, in 1936, California was advertising for teachers with degrees.

Holding her place in the book with her finger, she remembered the night the Anderson family had made the decision to move. Her father had gone to the telephone exchange to call his brother in California. When he'd gotten back, the family had met him at the front door.

"What did Will say, Stanley?" her mother asked anxiously.

Her father's eyes had been misty. "Sarah, he said we'd be welcome to stay in his home until we get a place of our own."

Sarah had dropped to the sofa as if her legs would no longer support her. "What a relief!"

"Tim, get Mother a glass of water," Clay said, and his eight-year-old brother had run to the kitchen. Always the family clown, tall, blond Clay snickered. "What's the matter, Mom? Scared Aunt Letitia would lock the door on us?"

Their mother's laugh had been tremulous. "Well, their social status is a little above ours. Their lavish Christmas cards told me that—until they stopped sending them. And don't forget, their daughter, Diane, is about ready for college. When they moved to San Francisco, you, Diane, and Emily were just babies."

So now, after all those years, Stanley and Will Anderson would meet again.

The bus hit a bump, and Emily closed her book and thought of the happy reunion. Or would the difference in their circumstances strain the relationship? After all, this wasn't just a casual visit.

The final blow in the Anderson financial crisis had struck with Tim's pneumonia. His hospital bills had taken every penny, including the payment for the mortgage they'd had to take out on their home. Even then, God had blessed them; Tim had survived.

She looked over the back of the seat ahead of her. Clay's brown eyes danced as he teased Tim, his tight lips holding back a grin.

"You must have been asleep. *I* saw it."

"Clay, are you telling the truth?" Tim asked warily.

"Yeah! It was the biggest jackrabbit I ever saw!"

"How do you know it was a jackrabbit?"

"Because he had long floppy ears and big long legs. He kept hopping ahead of the bus, waiting for us to catch up!"

Tim's hazel eyes fastened on Clay's with a dubious smile. Passengers around them chuckled at Clay's teasing, and suddenly Emily felt sorry for her cousin Diane. How lonely she must be without brothers like Tim and Clay. Though three years younger, Clay was Emily's closest friend.

Outside the bus stops along the highway, in lean-tos or tents, Indians displayed turquoise jewelry, clay pottery, and handcrafts that seemed unique to the Andersons. The bus was slowing for one of those rest stops now. Emily scanned the upcoming scene and wondered how Native Americans subsisted in such a harsh environment. Had any ever chosen to move to an urban area where life was easier?

She gasped, ashamed of herself. She'd assumed they wanted the life she knew, when in reality, the Indians might be wondering why the sweltering bus passengers chose to travel, crammed like sardines, in a diesel-driven motor coach!

❧

Hank Garrett hopped out of the car, called a thank-you to the driver who had given him a ride, and wished *he* were a passenger on the San Francisco-bound bus parked at the stop. He made his way through the passengers, Indians, and locals into the small adobe cafe.

A throaty feminine laugh induced Hank to search for its owner. His gaze fell upon a vision with shiny brown hair, blue eyes, and full pink lips, seated at a rickety pedestal table near the door. Four others, members of her family, he decided, crowded closely around the table with her. Each ordered a five-cent hamburger, and the father picked out two oranges from a basket on the counter and cut them in sections to be shared.

The little boy gobbled up his hamburger and orange section, and the pretty girl smiled. "Tim, would you like the rest of my hamburger? I'm not as hungry as I thought."

"Now, you must eat too, dear," said a small, older woman with streaks of gray in her wavy brown hair. "You've shared your food with one of the boys every time we've eaten. You finish your sandwich this time. I'll share."

The slightly built man who had sliced the orange waggled his forefinger. "This is not a picnic, Tim. You may have some more orange, but that's all. I'll give you a peppermint later."

"Okay, Dad."

That family must be saving every penny, thought Hank. The girl was willing to sacrifice part of her tiny lunch for the little boy. Choosing a counter stool when he came in, Hank had ordered a large hamburger with French fries. Now he felt ashamed. On the other hand, as they talked and laughed, there was a warmth about the family that made him envious. He'd never had that. Hank smiled when the girl caught his longing glance and blushed.

Too soon, the boarding call brought the family to their feet to catch the bus. Hank rose and followed at a discreet distance to watch them leave. Waiting her turn to step up into the coach, the girl hesitated, glanced back, and looked directly at Hank. The look was magic. He wanted to buy a bus ticket, to get on and follow her, but he couldn't. He couldn't let his editor down. He had to keep going.

He reentered the cafe as the cook set his lunch on the counter and reluctantly recalled why he was there. Assigned by the *Chronicle* in San Francisco to write a series of stories on America's poverty-stricken, he had started with the migrant workers in California. Next, he'd joined a wheat-harvest gang in the Midwest. Now, he would discover how the Depression was affecting Native Americans. The livelihood of those tribes came mainly from tourist trade, but travelers these days could hardly feed themselves, much less buy Indian goods.

He had a friend at the bus station in Frisco. He'd nailed down stories with a lot less information than he had on the beautiful girl he'd seen. If it was possible, and it would be, he'd locate her.

৵৹

Her parents suffered badly from the heat, so Emily was grateful for the cool twilight. Opening the novel she had almost finished, she settled back in the corner of the seat to read a little more. A new image of the story's hero emerged. He had the black hair and intelligent brown eyes of the handsome stranger she'd seen at the bus stop in the desert. Her face warmed at her imagining, and she forced the image from her mind.

Route 66 took them through Gallup, New Mexico. Indians in picturesque dress roamed the streets and possessed Tim's thoughts until he went to sleep. The family changed buses at Barstow, California, and stayed on a westerly route through the foothills of the Tehachapi Mountains. Leaving behind the desert and the Joshua trees, they headed north. Soon, San Francisco!

Drawn into the ambiance of California, Tim had his family rubbernecking to glimpse his wonders as well as their own. "Look at that mountain, Emily!" Tim almost shouted. "It's really high, isn't it? I'd like to climb clear to the top."

Tim was sitting with her, now. Emily peered over his shoulder. Mountains were a curiosity to a family from the plains state of Kansas, and the temperate climate and profuse growth of flowers and vegetables seemed a miracle to them all.

Sarah was fascinated by California's tall, heavily laden date palms. "Can't you just taste them? Seems ages since we could afford such things. I wonder if they're cheap out here? And oranges! Do you think we'll see orange groves?" she asked Stanley. Emily looked across the aisle at her parents, and her heart lightened at the sound of their happy voices. *Please, Lord, let this work. They've been through enough,* she prayed.

Her father had been the loan officer at the Brewster Bank until it closed. Placed in a job with the Works Progress Administration, Stanley Anderson had worked on a road gang until his decision to move his family to California. The WPA job had been humiliating, but Stanley had never complained, and he'd exhorted his family to keep their faith strong. "Remember what Paul said in the first chapter of Colossians: 'That ye might walk worthy of the Lord unto all pleasing, being fruitful in every good work, and increasing in the knowledge of God.' That will be our goal, and God will work it out to his glory."

We're waiting, God, Emily thought. *Show us what to do.*

A glimpse of the magnificent blue-green Pacific Ocean heralded the Andersons' arrival at their new home. The bus wound around, over steep hills and down narrow streets, to park in a space adjacent to the crowded, old-fashioned depot. Out of respect for the anxious passengers behind them, the Andersons filed quickly out of the bus.

With the commotion of luggage and bus passengers being loaded or unloaded, the scene around them shifted and stirred like wild currents in a rushing stream. Emily and her family clustered close as her father's eyes searched the crowd for the one face he'd recognize.

"Stanley! Here!" Will pushed his ample form through the crowd of passengers until he stood in front of them. The men shook hands then grabbed each other in a bear hug. "You're here, at last," Will finished, a sob in his voice.

"Never thought it would happen, Will," Stanley said, taken by sentiment. He laughed as he scratched his head. "If I'd known how hot that desert was, I'm not sure we'd be here now!"

Will Anderson was not what Emily had expected. He was the younger of the two brothers, but he looked much older than her dad. He had the same salt-and-pepper hair, but his hairline had receded and lines creased his forehead. Compared to her father's soft features that spoke of a kind heart, a hint of austerity clouded Will's gaze. Having barely known Clay, and Tim not at all, Will welcomed them politely then proceeded to flatter Sarah and Emily.

"You haven't changed an iota, Sarah. Same lovely blue eyes and same lovely hair. Hardly any gray at all. Stanley's a lucky man." Will smiled. "As for Emily—I can't think of anyone, except my Diane, who even comes close. You're a very pretty girl." Removing and sliding his wire-rimmed glasses into his vest pocket, he rubbed his hands together. "Well! We'll certainly have some excitement now! Four young people in the house instead of one."

By the time Will finished, his expression had changed and his hands dropped to his sides. Emily thought it was a look of distress, and she hoped she was wrong. Was it possible Uncle Will was not as overjoyed at their coming as her father had thought? They planned to stay at his house until they found jobs, but her dad had too much pride to linger where their presence was a burden.

With the assistance of a tall, big-boned man whom Will

did not introduce, the luggage was loaded into a second car. Tim sat on Clay's lap when the astonished family packed into Will's splendid black automobile. The mid-afternoon traffic was light, Will said, though there was more traffic than Brewster, Kansas, saw in a month. They arrived at Will's huge house in Ingleside Terrace sooner than Emily expected, and the appearance of the house and grounds was a shock to everyone.

Veering off the route to the garage lay a circular drive that led past the main entry. The Spanish-style dwelling, roofed with red tile, was two stories high and stood proudly sheltered by giant old scrub oaks. On the front lawn, twin fountains sprayed sparkling water into elevated pools surrounded by coral roses, white lilies, and blue irises. A veranda ran along the front and one side of the house, its length accommodating precisely placed brick-colored lounge chairs. Two luxuriant Boston ferns occupied wicker stands on either side of the elaborately carved double doors of the main entry.

At the back of the house, where they climbed out of the car, lay a spacious lawn bordered with blooming roses. Above them, climbing plants, which Will called bougainvillea, exploded with purple blossoms on white trellises. Comfortable lawn chairs, shaded with large green umbrellas, were randomly set in groups of two or three.

The luggage was transferred from the cars to the wide screened-in porch where two women waited inside at the back door. "Here's my little family!" Will boomed, and with a giant smile he introduced Letitia and Diane.

But no one touched or shook hands as Emily thought they would. Eyeing the stack of luggage, Letitia welcomed them with fluttering hands, her small gray eyes sliding back and forth between the five of them. Diane said nothing beyond a terse "hello." Petite, blond, dressed fashionably in a sailor-style dress, she examined her aunt, uncle, and cousins with a detached air.

Inside, Emily viewed opulence she'd never known existed. A shining, well-equipped kitchen lay off the hall to the right, and a small Chinese man in a white jacket and cap prepared vegetables at a glossy porcelain sink with silver faucets. Continuing down the wide hallway, Emily peeked into the dining room with its long gleaming table and high-back chairs padded with red velvet. A cranberry vase of fresh flowers sat on a buffet, the only other piece of furniture she could see from the hall.

The next opening was the archway to a living room twice the size of theirs at home. In fact, the house in Kansas would have fit nicely inside this one with space left over. The stairway, where Will directed them, lay to the left of the arched door. Mindful of the woodwork and walls, the men lugged their belongings upstairs to the rooms Letitia had assigned.

Clay and Tim's large room overlooked the backyard. A similar room with a little balcony was allotted to Sarah and Stanley, and it adjoined the boys' quarters. Emily had suspected she would share Diane's room. But she was wrong. Letitia led her to an upstairs room at the front of the house.

"I think you'll be comfortable here," she said. "I know it hasn't the frills Diane's room boasts, but I do like the candlewick bedspread and drapes, don't you?"

"It's lovely, Aunt Letitia," said Emily, wondering how much nicer Diane's room could be than the one before her. From the colorful rag rugs to the four-poster bed, crystal lamps, and pastel throw pillows, the room was lavishly decorated. "I hope someday we can repay you for welcoming us as you have."

Letitia's hands fluttered to her short-cropped graying hair. "You just conduct yourself like a lady, as much as possible, and we'll consider that payment enough."

Leaving a surprised and confused Emily, Letitia tiptoed from the room. She had hardly gone when Clay brought in Emily's suitcases. When she didn't acknowledge his presence, he dropped both bags on the floor with a thud.

"What's the matter? Homesick already?"

"No," she said, looking past him at nothing. "I just had a short but strange conversation with our aunt."

"Oh, yeah? What did she say?" Clay gave her his complete attention.

Emily repeated the exchange verbatim. "Can you imagine what she meant?"

Clay hesitated then lightened the air with a smile. "Far be it from me to say, but don't let me catch you swinging on that crystal chandelier in the dining room."

Giggling, Emily whacked his arm. "I'll try not to embarrass you *or* Aunt Letitia." Emily sat on the dressing table stool, unbuckled her sandals, and stepped out of them. "What do you have in mind for tomorrow? Jobwise, I mean."

Combing his hair in her dressing table mirror, Clay said, "I'll take a look at the paper first, then go down to the Embarcadero. Dad says a lot goes on there. I might be able to pick up work repairing boat engines."

"That sounds like a good idea. Your part-time experience at Hanley's garage should help." She jostled him aside to check her own hair. "As for me, I have to get a line on the board of education right away, but I'm tired. I'd like to rest a day before I begin." He elbowed her and finished combing his hair.

"Not me. I want to get into stuff as soon as I can."

"Watch your conduct," Emily joked as he went out the door.

❧

Following dinner that evening came hours of family discussion, some enlightening, some disheartening. Will was not as optimistic about the men's job possibilities as Stanley and Clay were. Although San Francisco had a port known around the world, the city was an important financial center, and oil refining and shipbuilding employed hundreds, men were begging for jobs. The influx of out-of-state unemployed had diminished job openings from many to almost nonexistent.

"Stanley, tomorrow I'll take you for a tour of my market building downtown," said Will. "Growers bring in truckloads of fresh produce every day. For a set fee, they can rent a stall to display their goods for sale to the public."

"That's very enterprising of them; and you, too, of course."

"Yes, I try to be civic-minded. Frugal buyers or those less fortunate can purchase quality vegetables and fruit at a lower price. I feel I'm looking out for the city's good."

"Will always has the good of the people at heart," parroted Letitia, surveying the room to make sure they all listened. Will rose and walked to a cigar box behind the glass doors of a breakfront. "Cigar, Stanley?" Slightly embarrassed at Stanley's refusal, he closed the door and turned to Diane. "Sweetheart, what do you have planned for Emily's entertainment tomorrow?"

"Oh, Daddy, I can't entertain her tomorrow. Mama and I both have responsibilities. She has an organizational meeting for her literary society, and I'm helping decorate for Jeannie Boyd's wedding shower." Diane's brown eyes clouded and her full red lips formed a pout. "I told you, Daddy."

Will pulled her into his arms and smoothed her sleek blond hair. "Now, that's all right, baby. Daddy just forgot."

Relaxing in an overstuffed chair, Emily made her own excuse. "I'm exhausted anyway, Diane. I really hadn't planned to do anything tomorrow. I'm sure Mother needs rest, too."

"Good! Then it's all worked out, Mama." Diane bounced a satisfied glance at her mother as she picked up a magazine.

"I would like to do some telephoning, tomorrow, while everyone is occupied," said Emily. "We must get Tim in school, even if it's only temporary, and have his records transferred if they require it. As for myself, I have to contact the board of education. I need to orient myself on the procedure to teach."

"You don't plan any long-distance calls, do you?" inquired Letitia with a pinched expression.

"No, Aunt Letitia. Just local calls."

Letitia made room on the sofa for Diane. "That's all right, then. Will you need someone to help you with the telephone?"

Tim giggled, but Clay was not amused. Emily saw the two reactions and lowered her gaze. She shifted the subject to transportation.

"I'll call the transit company and get the streetcar and interurban schedules, too. Learning to get around the city will be a necessity for all of us," she murmured thoughtfully.

"You're a bright girl, Emily," observed Will as if surprised. "I doubt if you'll have trouble finding work."

"Emily graduated from college with honors only this month," said Stanley. "We're very proud of her."

Diane put down her magazine. "I could go to college, but I prefer to prepare myself for marriage. When the right man comes along, I want to be ready."

"As we want you to be, dear," Letitia fawned in a raised, high-pitched voice. "She's so popular, we almost need an appointment book to keep track of her social engagements."

Diane lowered her head modestly, sneaking a peek at Emily and Clay to see if they were watching. Emily hoped Clay's sigh of disgust went unnoticed. Suddenly, the sound of falling dominoes shattered the silence. All eyes turned to Tim.

"Goodness! That was noisy!" carped Letitia.

Sarah hurried to her son and, whispering, helped him return the dominoes to the box and put them away.

"Want to see my room, Emily?" asked Diane, motioning toward the hall as if defying Emily to refuse.

Emily followed Diane down the hall to a room that had been closed off when they came into the house. She wasn't at all prepared. Emily felt she was entering a fairyland.

Windows, chairs, a couch, and a canopy bed were decorated in a matching floral sateen piped with white satin. The blues and pinks of the pattern were picked up in accessories and pillows. A long room next to her bedroom contained a blue combination bath and dressing room, something seen only in a picture show. Emily was sure the suite had been professionally decorated.

A white telephone rang on a table beside her bed, and Diane dashed to answer.

"Yes?" She paused. "No, I couldn't go. Some of Daddy's relatives from Kansas came in, and he wanted me home," she said, her voice belittling Emily's value as a relative.

Emily signaled to leave, and Diane responded with a careless wave. In the hall, Emily gave in to despair. Snide remarks were not what she had expected from her father's family. She had hoped for a warm friendship between them. Will Anderson's wife and daughter lived surrounded by luxury. *In view of God's gifts,* Emily thought, *how sad that gratitude to Him had not produced happier attitudes.* How would she and her family fit in?

two

Clay left the big house early the next morning. He was not shy about asking directions, and using his first cable cars, he arrived at the Embarcadero within the hour. As expected, the place was alive with activity.

The Embarcadero, a crescent-shaped street, accommodated piers and wharves that lined the shore for three and a half miles. The west side was strung with stores and lodgings that sailors and longshoremen frequented. For a moment, Clay envied those men their freedom to travel as they wished, but only for a moment.

Brightly painted boats, mostly blue, tugged gently at their anchors and moorings along Fisherman's Wharf.

Clay wandered the wharf until he came upon a grizzled old man from whose ears hung large gold earrings. "I wonder who owns these boats?" he questioned. "Can you tell me?"

Deftly mending a net with a wooden needle, the man motioned toward a blue boat. "My grandsons own that one. The rest, the colorful ones, belong to the men from my country—Italy. We are the best! We are better than any skipper afloat because we deliver the biggest and the best catch."

He and Clay spoke only a few moments before the quiet scene changed. Fishing boats docked; their owners, including the Italians, haggled over prices with zealous buyers on the wharf. Clay tried but couldn't follow the process in the din of voices and accents. Finally waving good-bye to the old man he'd talked to, Clay continued to explore.

Restaurants in the area advertised seafood "caught today." Along the Taylor Street sidewalk, stands were set up to sell cooked fish. Huge iron cauldrons boiled fresh-caught crabs, clams, and other shellfish, which were sold to regular customers and to the workers in the area. Clay sampled a tidbit or two. They were delicious!

"First time in Frisco, kid?" a brawny worker asked, eyeing Clay and pausing to suck the meat from a crab leg.

Clay chuckled. "First time anywhere. Name's Clay." He held out his hand.

"Slider's my handle." The man wiped his palm on his pants and shook hands. "You bein' new and all, you need someone to show you the town, teach you some savvy for the big city."

"Do you work here?"

"Yep. Loading that ship over there." He pointed to a big black ship with a Russian flag then examined Clay silently.

"Must be a great life down here, in the thick of things."

"It could be—if they'd treat us right," muttered Slider.

"What do you mean?"

"You ain't from around here, are you?"

"No. From back East. . .Kansas."

"Oh, ho! No wonder you think it's 'a great life down here.' You shoulda been here in '34 when we tried to strike fer better pay and rights. It got real nasty. Rich people runnin' things don't want us little guys to have a decent life. They want to keep it all fer thurselves. They called out the police, and we had to fight back. And we'll do it again if we have to!"

"But don't people get hurt when you fight back?"

Slider removed his skullcap and slapped it back on. "Sure they do. That's what happens when you fight fer your rights. We need tough unions, so we don't have to fight. It's comin'.

You'll see. We're gettin' better organized all the time."

Clay listened with rapt attention. "You belong to a union?"

"Sure thing. How about you?"

"I just got here. I'm looking for work."

A big smile exposed Slider's missing tooth. "I might be able to put in a good word fer you. You'd have to join our union, though."

"That's all right. I don't care what I have to do. I need a job," said Clay.

"That's what we like to hear. 'Course it will cost you dues when your paychecks start comin' in."

"Just so they start coming. I don't mind."

Slider laid his arm across Clay's shoulders. "Let's go talk to some of the big boys. I'll introduce you around. First thing you know, you'll be callin' San Francisco home instead of that no-man's-land back East."

Clay strode along with Slider, confident he had happened on to the one guy who could get him in with the right people.

❧

Hank Garrett pushed his hat back and watched the two men enter the fishing gear shop. *So that's how they do it,* he thought, *pull them in gently once they find a vulnerable spot.* He'd bet anything the conversation he'd overheard was leading to an invitation to join the Communist Party.

As a newspaperman Hank also belonged to a union, but there was no hint of infiltration by that unwelcome gang. Hank wanted to uncover unions that encouraged the movement. Seeing the naïve kid taken in today was a repeat of what he'd seen many times, and unsavory characters showed up regularly at the shop where the boy had gone. He ordered a cup of coffee at the stall nearest him.

Hank had spent days on the Embarcadero, trying to get an

angle on the unrest rumbling between workers and their employers. No bloodshed had occurred, but attempts to form a conciliatory body to settle differences on the docks were at a standstill.

A ship signaled departure and Hank turned for a quick look. Then he focused on the shop again.

His stock was high at the *Chronicle* right now. His copy, stories of poverty-stricken America, had paid off. When he'd gotten back to the office, his editor had been so satisfied he'd given Hank a raise. These days, that was a miracle.

When he'd landed the job at the paper six years ago, his parents had doubted he could make good as a newsman. After this latest swing around the United States, he'd gone to Los Angeles to see his family. He wanted to break the news of his success, tell them about the raise, and boast a little. The trip had hiked his ego, but his success had brought him no closer to his family.

However, there was a hidden dividend to that countrywide jaunt: the girl in Arizona he couldn't forget. His friend, a cop on duty at the bus depot, had noticed the same girl Hank had seen. A lucky break! Her party had been met in San Francisco, and his friend had jotted down the license number of the car. He would find her. It was just a matter of time.

This story was the important thing now. The meeting he'd seen and overheard might be a direct lead to the dockworkers' problems, or it might be a lead to a different, better story. Once aware of all the possibilities, his instincts would clue him in on the right article. Settling himself on a box in the shade, eyes focused on the shop door, he waited for the boy to reappear.

≈

Clay smiled as he left the shop. Uncle Will and his dad would never believe he was this close to a job on his first day. It wasn't a sure thing, but Slider had taken him back to the office, to the owner of the fishing-gear shop. A few of his buddies were there, but none of them could compare to *the man*. Dressed in a slick business suit and fancy two-toned shoes, he was far more sophisticated than the others. His fingernails were buffed to a shine, and he was wearing a nice cologne. His name was Maroni. *Mister* Fred Maroni, he was called.

All Clay had to do, he said, was wait a couple of days until the union boss got back. Then he would most likely have a job. He hadn't told Clay what kind of job, but Slider hinted that he might use his mechanical skills. Clay thought he had it in the bag.

With a light heart, he quickened his pace and headed for the stall where he'd sampled the seafood. He ordered a full portion for his lunch. The old man at the shelf of the lean-to was pouring coffee for a tanned guy in slacks and a sport shirt.

"Wanna cup?" the old man held up his blackened coffeepot.

Clay nodded and watched until his cup was full.

As the other customer turned his head, Clay noticed a card stuck in his hatband with the word *press* barely showing.

"Thanks," he said, handing over another nickel. Curious, Clay turned. "I see your press card. Are you a real reporter? I mean, do you work for a San Francisco newspaper?"

The man chuckled. "I don't always get a *scoop,* if that's what you're thinking, but the *Chronicle* pays me to do my best."

The coffee Clay sipped burned going down. "I couldn't write, but I admire you guys who do. My sister likes to write. She's a teacher."

"Not an old-maid schoolteacher?" Hank spoke the words with a grin, and Clay came to her defense.

"Not her. She graduated from college this summer, and now she's looking for a job out here. *She* won't be an old maid."

"Pretty, eh?" Hank hiked his foot up on a broken packing crate. "Are you and she new to California?"

"Yeah, our whole family is. I'm down here looking for a job. I may have one," he said, puffing out his chest a little.

"Is that right? You're lucky. Jobs are hard come by."

"You're not kiddin'. That's why we came to California. Things were going from bad to worse in Kansas."

"Kansas?" asked Hank, looking for a way to draw him out.

"Yeah. I know what you're thinking—the dust bowl, as everybody's calling it. Well, it's true." Clay finished his coffee and crab and wiped his fingers on the paper wrapper. "We sold everything we had to get out here. We're staying with relatives now, but once Dad and I get jobs we'll have our own place."

Hank's mind was traveling ninety miles an hour. What if he followed up the *poverty* articles with one of a particular family migrating to California to escape the misery of the dust bowl? He could do both stories at once—one, a story about the family, and, the other, probing the inner recesses of the union the boy was expected to join. The boy could be the key to both.

"Tell you what. My name's Hank Garrett," he said, reaching in his pocket. He wrote on a bit of paper from a notepad. "I'd pay ten dollars to interview you and your family about why you left Kansas and the details of your trip to settle out here. Would you be interested? Think they would?"

"Would we? I'll make 'em be interested. Ten dollars is ten dollars!" Clay chortled.

ॐ

Clay and Hank talked for an hour, and when Clay got home, only his family was there. Stanley had just come in, and the

Chinese man, Lee, offered them tea and showed them to an informal eating area attached to the kitchen.

"Clay," Tim whispered, overjoyed, "I'm sure glad we don't have to eat in that prissy dining room every time."

Lee, normally unsmiling, chuckled, his dark eyes twinkling with merriment. But there the humor ended. No job had turned up for Stanley, so Clay's morning on the Embarcadero was the topic of interest. Lee brought their tea, and Clay sprang his big surprise.

"Wait'll I tell you my news! I met a guy by the name of Hank Garrett, and he wants to 'interview' our whole family. He's a reporter for a newspaper. He'll pay us ten dollars!"

Emily almost choked on her tea. "A reporter? Clay! I hope you haven't bitten off more than *we* can chew. Why would a newspaper reporter want to talk to us?"

"He called us 'fugitives from the dust bowl.' He's been reporting on what the Depression has done to people around the country. He'd like to write what he called a human-interest story about us. It's because it kinda wraps up what he's been doing. He could show what happened to a family that actually made the move to California." He leaned back with a proud look.

"Clay, wait a minute. I'm as skeptical as Emily," said Stanley, glancing quickly at Sarah, who nodded. "This doesn't sound like a story I'd like to be mixed up in. We aren't objects of pity, and the article might embarrass Will and Letitia."

Emily's face warmed as she remembered Aunt Letitia's warning that she be a lady at all times. Being written up in a newspaper might bring shame on them all. What if he wasn't a reporter and simply wanted to get inside the Anderson mansion?

"What paper does he work for, Clay?"

"The *Chronicle*."

"Wait a minute. Let's find out for sure." Emily rose and was back from the living room in minutes. Sinking into her chair, she clasped her hands on the table. "I called the paper. Hank Garrett *does* work for the *Chronicle*. The front desk says he's one of their best."

"I told you!" said Clay. "Hank Garrett is a swell guy! Wait 'til you meet him." He pulled Hank's number from his pocket. "All I have to do is call this number and tell him when to come out."

Sarah spoke seriously. "Stanley, we must talk to Letitia and Will about this. It's their home. We can't encumber them with a situation they may not care for. Hank Garrett or no Hank Garrett, they should know about this before we say another word."

Her mother was right; Emily was relieved. Clay would have to calm his eagerness to be written up as a "fugitive from the dust bowl" in the daily news. At this point, she wouldn't care if she never heard the words *Hank Garrett* again!

❧

"Hank Garrett!" exclaimed Will as they took their seats at the dining table that evening. "The feature writer with the *Chronicle?*"

"I don't know if that's what he is or not," replied Clay. "I asked him if he was a reporter, and he said he was."

Will leaned back with a big smile. "Regardless, Hank Garrett has a reputation in this town."

"Yes, Daddy. And he's so handsome!" crooned Diane, pressing her hands dramatically to her heart. "His picture was in the paper with a story about some homeless people, and he's divine."

He may be handsome, thought Emily, *but that name is driving me crazy!* She had heard it from Clay at least a dozen times since he'd gotten home from the Embarcadero. She wished he weren't so impressed with him. And the one he called Slider. What kind of a name was that?

Something bothered her about the whole morning. She wished to talk to her dad about it, but she didn't want to hurt Clay's feelings. She loved and trusted her brother, yet even a loyal Christian man like Clay could be taken in by a charlatan who was slick enough. Was Slider one of those?

"I don't suppose it would do any harm to invite your friend over for a meal, Clay," Will said. "Who knows? He might even mention the market in the interview." He waited while Lee placed an excellent crown roast in front of him. Without turning, Will said, "Fair job, Lee."

Stoically bowing, Lee colored slightly. The callous remark was not lost on Emily. Clay missed it. He was looking at his family for their reaction to Will's approval.

"I guess it's up to you, Dad," he said. "Do you want to let Hank do a story on us?"

"I'm still contemplating, Clay. A story of this kind would be very personal. Do we want San Francisco to know how poor we were when we came to this city? I don't intend to remain poor. Almost bragging about not having money doesn't seem honorable."

"I agree," said Emily crossly. "Who does this Hank Garrett think he is? We're private citizens, not freaks. How do we know what he would actually write about us?"

Clay spoke to allay her fears. "Oh! I forgot to tell you. Hank said we could read what he writes before his story goes to press."

"Well, then, I don't see any problem at all," said Will,

whom Emily suspected wanted to share the reporter's celebrity.

Diane's eyes sparkled with enthusiasm. "Good, Daddy! I'm *dying* to meet him. You probably won't like him, Emily, so I know we can't change your mind," she said with a cunning smile. "Try to be as nice as you can, anyway."

≥•

Two days later, Emily had her first encounter with San Francisco proper, and the day began badly. After being shuffled from office to office, she had no success with the board of education. Though her excellent transcript had been received with letters of recommendation, they regretted they had no openings but would keep her application on file.

Hurt, trying to keep from crying, Emily escaped to the hall. She wondered how she would break the bad news to her family.

I need You, Lord, she prayed. *Help me to keep trusting that You are in control and that jobs and a home are out there for us if we're patient. Please be with me as I tell my family they aren't hiring any more teachers.*

She heard someone at the office door and opened her eyes. A pixielike, red-haired girl dressed in green stood before her.

"You were praying, weren't you?" It was the young clerk Emily had met in the administration office.

"Yes," said Emily, wiping her eyes. "I was so sure I'd get a job this morning, I'm asking God's forgiveness for being too self-absorbed and not abiding in Him."

The girl's smile was warm. "I understand. My name's Celia Grant. I'm a Christian, too."

"I'm Emily Anderson. But I guess you already knew that."

Celia's face colored. "I remembered your face but not your name." She held up a brown paper bag and shook it. "I've got an extra sandwich in here. Would you come to a little nearby park and eat with me? I'd like to get better acquainted with you. I might be able to help."

three

Many working people were also eating in the downtown park where the girls shared Celia's lunch. In the shade of a grove of silver-dollar poplars, Emily and Celia found an iron bench and, carefully tearing open the sack, used it to spread the lunch between them. There were two sandwiches, two cookies, but only one orange, and Celia asked questions as she peeled and divided the orange.

"We moved from Kansas, and my family and I need to find jobs and a home right away," Emily answered.

"Where are you living now?" Celia set the two halves of the orange on their makeshift table.

"With Dad's brother and his family. They're nice enough, but we've always had our own home, and it's strange, living with someone else. We need jobs, Celia—Dad, Clay, and I."

Celia swallowed a bite of her egg-salad sandwich. "Who's Clay?" she asked, handing Emily a napkin while Celia dabbed at her mouth with her hankie.

"My little brother." Emily laughed softly. "Only he's not so little. He's about six feet tall."

"How old is he? What does he look like?" her friend probed with an interested expression.

"He's nineteen, and he's a big tease. I guess you could call him handsome. He doesn't have any *bad* features, but he's not one of those glamour boys like Clark Gable." Emily cocked her head to the side and squinted one eye. "I guess he looks more like a sandy-haired James Stewart, if you don't look too closely." She laughed again.

Celia chuckled. "He sounds heavenly. My age, too."

"Before you start thinking he's better than he is, let me warn you that Clay is not the refined type. He's an out-of-work mechanic looking for a job. Any job."

"Which brings us back to why I wanted to talk to you." Celia brushed a bread crumb from her skirt. "Loretta, my sweet sister-in-law, just told us that one of her teachers quit because her husband was called to pastor a church up North. Loretta is principal of a small Christian school. It doesn't pay much, and it's first grade—you know, the little scared ones. But if you're anxious for a job, it's better than nothing."

Emily let out a long breath. "It sounds better than anything! I'm a first-grade teacher!"

"Do you mean it?"

"Yes! I could do it! I'm experienced!"

Celia jumped to her feet. "Then let's get back to the office and I'll call Loretta. If she's free this afternoon, I'll give you directions, and you can go over there now."

Two hours later, gratefully thanking God, Emily had the job.

ð

After arriving home and telling her mother and Aunt Letitia the good news, Emily went right upstairs to her room. She could hardly wait to have a bath after her exhausting day. Afterward, she looked at her meager wardrobe and felt heartsick. It was a disaster! She settled on a blue shirtwaist dress with a white collar and hoped it was appropriate for dinner and the interview with their renowned guest.

The house sparkled. Emily had seen Aunt Letitia's cleaning people leaving as she came in. Apparently her aunt and uncle thought nothing too good for Hank Garrett, the feature writer.

Diane was nowhere to be seen, and Emily suspected she was shopping for something new to dazzle the guest. She was right. When Emily came down in her old cotton shirtwaist, Diane was showing the older women a sleek, navy linen dress. The purchase also included blue-and-white spectator pumps. Emily adored shoes and, though she knew she shouldn't, she envied Diane. The white, high-heel sandals Emily was wearing seemed bulky and out of vogue.

Stanley and Clay came in shortly before Will, and her father was in low spirits. No job yet. He and Sarah went to their room to freshen up for dinner, and Emily wondered what words her mother would use to cheer him up. Sarah Anderson had a wealth of experience in turning dark moods around.

Ordinarily Stanley was a rock, but, since his termination at the bank, Emily had seen her dad go through much that would be difficult for any Christian man, even a Christian as strong as Stanley Anderson.

Emily lowered herself into an occasional chair and bowed her head in prayer. *Father God, I thank You for the job You've given me today and for peace of mind. I know it's just a matter of patience to wait for the jobs You have for Dad and Clay. Please, Lord, help Dad know we have faith in him. The perfect job You've provided is out there, waiting for him. Let this evening go well for all our sakes, Father. Don't let this man make a fool of us in print, and give Clay wisdom to choose the right friends. In Jesus' name, amen.*

She raised her head. The house was silent. Everyone was busy with preparations for the evening except her, and though she had asked, her help was not needed. Lee was assisted in the kitchen by a tiny Chinese woman—his wife?—on this night of visiting royalty.

No one ever played the piano tucked in a corner of the big

living room, so Emily strolled over and lifted the lid of the bench to see what music it contained. Buried under a double stack of popular sheet music, she found a Chopin étude and a book of Clementi. She took out the étude, began to play, and had entered into the mood of the piece when the doorbell rang.

No one came to answer. Surely her aunt or uncle would appear. Emily stopped playing and listened. Quick footsteps came from the inner recesses of the house, and the Chinese woman shuffled timidly toward the door. She hesitated when she saw Emily, who stood, tilted her head, and smiled. The woman smiled back and walked confidently to open the door.

"How do you do?" a deep, hidden voice greeted. "My name is Hank Garrett. Are Mr. and Mrs. Anderson at home?"

Emily saw the little woman lose confidence again. Probably too much English too fast. Emily stepped forward to rescue her.

"I'm Emily Anderson," she said. "We're expecting you. Won't you come in?" She smiled again at the servant, who needed only that to quit the room.

❧

Hank Garrett's legs would hardly support him. It was her! The girl at the bus stop in Arizona! Only she wasn't in Arizona. She was standing in front of him, an arm's length away! The same shining hair, the outrageous blue eyes, a pert nose that begged a little kiss, pink lips that framed a smile to destroy a man's heart—they were all there in the same sweet package he remembered. He couldn't formulate a coherent sentence. She was carrying on her part of a polite conversation, and he was struck dumb!

The young lady smiled devastatingly. "My brother Clay has been telling us all about you, Mr. Garrett. He admires you, to say the least."

So this was Clay's sister No. She definitely would not be an old-maid schoolteacher.

ಇಎ

The man is exasperating, thought Emily. Was he being rude, or was he merely shy? He'd stared at her since he stepped inside the door yet had not uttered a word. She was running out of things to say.

"I'm sure everyone will be here in a moment. Would you have a seat, please? I'll get one of the men." Emily headed for the stairs.

Hank Garrett dropped into a chair, still staring.

What's so familiar about our guest? Emily wondered. And who first coined the phrase "tall, dark, and handsome"? Whoever she was, she must have had this guy in mind. In a dress suit, crisp white shirt, and tie, he made all other men look tacky. *Work clothes,* why was she thinking *work clothes?* They hadn't met, yet there was just something. . . Deep in thought, she nearly collided with her uncle at the landing on the staircase.

"Uncle Will, Mr. Garrett is here. I was just coming to tell you."

"Clay's ready. You get him, and I'll go down and keep our visitor company," he said, fastening the buttons on his suit coat.

Minutes later Emily and her family joined the two men as Letitia and Diane came from their rooms. Diane stared and giggled when she was introduced, and Letitia's hands fluttered a path from her hair to her collar and back again. Stanley and Sarah were gracious, as Emily knew they would be, but it was a courtesy mixed with characteristic reserve. Hank Garrett would get *nothing* from them that would embarrass the family.

"Hank, I'm glad you could come!" said Clay. "We've been

looking forward to this, haven't we, folks?" Clay looked toward Will and Diane, since they were the most eager to invite Hank.

Instantly, Diane agreed. "Oh, yes! We've been waiting to meet the great Hank Garrett of the *Chronicle*. We're so excited to have a famous reporter as our dinner guest. Mama and Daddy have done everything possible to make your visit enjoyable, haven't you, dears?" she simpered, batting eyes heavy with mascara.

Letitia nodded nervously in the background as Will bestowed his blessing, "We certainly want you to feel welcome, Hank. Why don't we all take a seat, and maybe you can tell us about some of the stories you're working on at the paper."

Hank opened his mouth, but Diane cut him off. "Daddy, dear, let's not bother him with questions about his work right now." She turned in her chair next to him and leaned forward. "I've never heard of a *Mrs.* Garrett. Are you married, Hank, or is that position still open?"

Will and Letitia laughed and listened for his answer. Emily clasped her hands, embarrassed, and noticed her family was uncomfortable, too. It was as though they were not there. Diane dominated the conversation, a foolish one, and her parents encouraged her. Emily now understood why Diane was always out with or talking on the phone to boys. She had a way of making a man forget there was any other girl in the room.

Emily felt her face flush. Was she jealous of a spoiled child playing up to an egotistical newspaperman? Absolutely not! *If only he would stop looking at me,* she thought. He, Diane, and Clay were laughing at an inane joke of Diane's, yet every few seconds Hank Garrett's eyes captured hers when they drifted in his direction.

Lee announced dinner, and, with the rest, Emily rose and

followed the small, gray-haired man to the dining room.
Grateful to slip quietly into her regular place, her face warmed
again when Hank was assigned a chair directly opposite her.
For the next hour, though Diane was seated beside him, talking nonstop, his riveting hazel-eyed gaze followed her every
move.

≈

Hank lowered his head, embarrassed. He could not stop
looking at Emily. What a dope! Out of an ordinary day had
come a miracle, and he was messing up like a kid.

He'd heard the piano when he parked in the drive, and he
was enthralled with the melodic presentation. Then, realizing
she was the pianist added another facet to her magnetism. He
had already compared her to music. When she spoke, the
sound was lyrical, and, when she smiled, a whole symphony
threw his heart out of rhythm.

She'd slipped away after he got there, and, once more in
command of his emotions, he had chatted with the uncle
until her entire family appeared together. And what a family!
Tim was a great kid, and he'd liked Clay from the first.
That's why he had this giant urge to protect him. With parents like Sarah and Stanley, the boys couldn't help growing
up right. Nothing should happen to change that now.

Which brought him back to Emily. Emily Anderson, the kind
of girl he'd like to marry—someday. A shock went through
him as his mind gave life to the thought.

"I just can't imagine how you think up all those wonderful
stories you write, Hank. When I read them I'm simply inspired
by your talent with words."

Dazzling Diane was a Victrola record he couldn't turn off.
But he had been invited to her parents' home, so he smiled
continually at her tittering nonsense and felt ridiculous. He

decided to add a little reality and inform the *whole* group.

"It's my job, and I went to college to learn it. After a while, and with a few breaks, a good reporter reaches the point where he can almost smell a good story." He was pushing it a little, but he wanted to impress Emily.

"Even then it must take scads of talent," trilled Letitia, clearly as much of a social fake as Diane. "We're delighted to have such an important writer as a guest in our home."

Hank glanced at Emily, then away, thinking that the other two women were as phony as any he'd ever encountered. He kept hoping Emily would ask about his work until it occurred to him he should be asking about hers. He rushed to correct the oversight.

"Will you be teaching this term, Emily?" he ventured, when Diane and Letitia chose food over flattery.

"Yes, but not in a public school. Fortunately, I met a very nice girl today. She steered me in the direction of the Ocean Gardens Christian School. I start teaching first grade there next week. God has been very good to me."

Sarah and Stanley Anderson smiled at Emily as if they knew something he didn't, and suddenly Hank was uncomfortable. Even Clay had the look as Hank watched him, and he wondered if it was the mention of God that got such a reaction.

Worshiping God was not one of Hank's priorities. In fact, people who filled their lives with that hogwash were a curiosity to him. Surely Emily wasn't one of those. She was too smart. She probably mentioned God to please her folks. Yes, that was it. Sure.

Yet, in his heart, though he'd rather not acknowledge it, he had a feeling he was dead wrong.

Back in the living room, Will offered his box of cigars to

the men. They refused, but he lit up his own.

"Nothing like a good cigar after dinner," he said, coughing, his face reddening. "Are you a native of San Francisco, Garrett?"

"No, I was born in Los Angeles. My parents and sister still live there."

"Hollywood!" exclaimed Diane. "Do they live in Hollywood? I've always wanted to go there and look at the movie stars' homes. I love motion pictures, don't you?" Moving closer to Hank, she addressed him in an undertone as if they were alone.

"I seldom go to a picture show," he declared to the rest. "Life, to me, is more exciting than any motion picture. Besides, I'm too busy most of the time." He glanced at Emily. "If I had a date, though, and she wanted to go—"

"*I'd* like to go with you, Hank," cut in Diane. "More than anything, I *love* motion pictures."

"Okay, maybe we could make it a party. Emily, would you and Clay and Tim be interested? We can see a double feature at the Rialto next week. Bette Davis and Fredric March are both on the bill."

Clay smiled, Diane frowned, and Emily tried to get out of it. "Why don't the three of you go?" she suggested. "I start teaching on Monday. I'll have lots of evening work to do, and Tim will need to get to bed early because of school."

"We'll wait until the week after, then," suggested Hank.

"Oh, no! I want to see those pictures," said Diane. "We can go without Emily. I'll tell her all about it when we get home. Please, Hank," she said, with the pout Emily had seen her use on Uncle Will.

Emily couldn't read Hank's faint smile. "All right," he said. "Would Wednesday night be all right with you, Clay?"

Clay looked at his parents and back at Hank. "I don't think—"

"Wednesday night is prayer meeting at church, Hank," said Stanley. "I'd hate Clay to miss our first one in California."

"So would I. Sorry, Hank," said Clay.

Stanley explained. "You see, we haven't joined a church yet, but I've spoken to the pastor of the one we'll visit. Prayer meeting is the best way to take the pulse of a church. If its heartbeat is Jesus Christ, that's the one we'll join."

Clay turned to Hank. "He's right. You and Diane go without us."

Trapped, thought Emily. Or would he enjoy it? Probably. In her heart she wanted to be with Hank, but something about him scared her. He was so worldly. He was glamorous, drove an open-air roadster, and probably had dozens of girls clamoring to date him. She was a first-grade teacher from Kansas.

She had dated only sons of friends of the family. Except for one pest, they had been nice. *Norman* was the son of Stanley's boss at the bank. When the bank reopened, he had taken her dad's old job. Stanley felt no malice; he was thankful for his road gang job. But Norman Conner had attached himself to Emily as if she should have felt honored that he chose her. Their move to California had solved the problem.

Emily heard Diane accept at once, and, in the background, Letitia's hands fluttered, and Will puffed away, both obviously pleased with the conquest. Hank's face told Emily nothing, but in a stiff, polite voice, he agreed to pick up Diane at seven o'clock the following Wednesday evening. Then, he gave Emily a quick glance.

"Have you seen anything of San Francisco yet?" he directed to her family. "For pleasure, I mean."

Stanley gave Will and Letitia a look of concern. "There's been no time for sight-seeing, Hank. Clay and I are trying our best to get jobs. We want a place of our own as soon as possible, so we can let Will's family get back to normal."

Will waved a hand. "Now, Stanley, there's no hurry. You're welcome for as long as you need to stay."

Letitia stopped fluttering and spoke up. "Now, Will, let *them* decide. I don't blame them for wanting a home of their own. Anyone would. I understand."

Aunt Letitia was a bit too eager. For Emily it confirmed the fact that she hadn't been as agreeable to their coming as Uncle Will made it seem.

Her concentration was disturbed by Hank's abrupt bid for their attention. "I wonder if we might finish the review of your experiences in the past few weeks, Mr. Anderson. We touched on useful information during dinner, but I need to ask a few questions and also get the chronological time line correct." He turned to Will. "Do you have any objection to our using your dining room for a private conference?"

"No. . .ah. . .no, not at all," Will replied.

Had Will thought they would all be in on the interview? Surely not. Who would want to hear a repetition of their sad, hard-times tale? Emily was reluctant to get into the details, herself. They were demeaning to the family.

She hoped Norman's name wouldn't be mentioned. But why not? Why should she care if Hank Garrett knew about him? She and Norman had parted friends. Moving toward the dining room, she heard Diane's voice behind them, whining to get her way.

"I don't see why they can't stay right here and talk."

Letitia's voice sounded as pouting as Diane's. "Don't be disappointed, dear. They won't be long, I'm sure."

Emily hoped she was right.

four

For a private two hours, Hank Garrett's inquiries took priority. Yet casual conversation did intervene, and Hank let it happen.

"Mr. Garrett—" Stanley started.

"Please, call me Hank."

"Sure I will, Hank." Stanley chuckled. "I admit, I was having trouble with that 'mister' business. Seems stiff and formal." He laid his forearm on the dining table and eyed Hank quizzically. "I heard you tell my brother you were from Los Angeles. Did you go to school there or in San Francisco?"

"I went to UCLA, sir, in Los Angeles. But I admired the editor of the *Chronicle* for his editorials and wasn't satisfied until I applied to work for him. Despite my father's efforts to thwart my leaving L.A., the editor hired me and gave me my first real break."

"You're happy here in San Francisco, then?" asked Sarah.

"Yes ma'am! There's a lot to like about this city. *Yerba Buena* was its name in the beginning. It was a happy community. People worked at building the Presidio when it was established and on the mission after Father Juníperro Serra arrived. Little by little the settlement grew and became important."

At the mention of Father Serra, Emily couldn't resist the conversation. "I promised myself I'd visit some of the missions along the coast since they're such an important part of California's history."

Eagerly, Hank turned toward her. "Have you heard about Mission Delores, right here in San Francisco?"

"I've heard of it, but I know nothing about it." Try as she might, Emily couldn't avoiding his entrancing eyes.

"May I take you there? You'd enjoy seeing the place. Even with a class of first graders, you'll be including a little history, and as you said, the missions are an important part of our history. What about going Sunday afternoon?"

"I don't know. . . ." Emily glanced nervously at her dad and mother, but they apparently missed her tension and offered no objection.

But Hank didn't miss it."Better still, what about taking Tim along?" he suggested. "He'll hear about the mission's history in school. A trip there would make it more real."

"Yeah, Emily! How about taking me?" Pleading with a smile, Tim jumped up and circled the table to Emily.

His enthusiasm won Emily's consent, and on Hank's face she caught a smile of satisfaction. She was the one trapped this time. But, again, Diane was the problem. How would she react if Hank came to the house to get Tim and her? There had to be another way.

"Hank, could I have a sheet of your notepad?" He tore one out for her. "We shouldn't leave from here, Dad. Diane. . . Why don't you give Hank the directions to the church, and he can meet us there after the service."

Her parents caught her reasoning at once, and Stanley began a makeshift map for the reporter.

"There's one more place you need to see," said Hank. "It's worth all the others and then some. The Golden Gate Bridge. I've been doing a series of articles on it, and it's an amazing structure."

Stanley straightened up from his map-drawing and smiled.

"I've been keeping up with it. First time I get the chance, I intend to take a gander at that thing."

Clay, who had been silent until now, liked the idea, too. "Count me in on that trip! It's the talk of the town."

"Can we go see it, Dad?" Tim asked, excited again.

Hank laughed. "We'll make sure you do, Tim." And he glanced at Emily, a suggestion in his eyes.

"You're a kind man, Hank," said Sarah. "When we get our own home, I'm going to bake you a cherry pie."

The rest of the Andersons laughed.

"You've made an impression!" said Stanley, and his face sobered. "Tell us, Hank, when did they start the bridge?"

"January of '33, although there was a ton of preliminary events before it happened. Once the people who promoted it got the interest of the city engineer, he sent out inquiries to engineers with the finest reputations, asking if they thought a bridge could be built across the strait.

"Joseph B. Strauss had built bridges for years, and he was the one who grasped the concept. The bridge was a dream he *believed* in. Not only did he believe in it, he had ways to convince the politicians, promote the bridge, and get the money. The counties affected got an act through the legislature, permitting them to organize ideas for what they felt was needed in the way of a bridge. But because of the port, they had to have the war department's authority to go ahead. Finally, the war department came through, and San Francisco and Marin counties were given a temporary okay."

"You mean it got done? Just like that?" asked Clay in surprise.

"Not by a long shot." Hank laughed. "The opposition was just getting started. The ferry companies didn't like it, and neither did those with special projects they thought were more important. Mr. Strauss was finally selected to head up the bridge's construction and the plan took life. He *made* it take life! The proposed cost was $35 million! When they brought up the bond issue to build, people voted *for* it, in the middle of hard times! You might say it was a miracle."

"I can't think how much money that is, but I'd like to see a bridge that cost that much!" declared Tim.

"Me, too!" Clay said, grinning.

Stanley put his hand on Tim's shoulder. "The money's impressive, Tim, but the *dream* was the important thing." He turned to Hank. "When you come after Emily and Tim, Sunday, why don't you get there in time for church? Clay or Emily could wait for you outside and bring you in to sit with us. We always get there early; it's a habit of ours. We'd be mighty glad to have you with us, Son."

His last word nearly convinced Hank to try it again. Maybe it would be different, especially if Emily was there. But he couldn't make himself say yes. He shook his head and lied. "Sorry, I'll probably have to work Sunday."

Everybody gives false excuses, don't they? he thought. But, this time, Hank didn't like himself. He forced a smile and led the family back to finish the interview. "Stanley, let me assure you there will be no article until you, Clay, and Emily are working, and you have a home of your own. And remember, you have the right to approve every line that goes to press."

The men shook hands, and Emily and Sarah observed the exchange, smiling.

Tim walked beside Hank as they returned to the living room. "I like you, Hank," he said. "You're a lot nicer to me than old Norman. He was a pain in the neck."

Chuckling, Hank ruffled Tim's hair. "Who's old Norman?"

"Oh, he's one of Emily's boyfriends back in Kansas. He never wanted me to go anywhere with them."

Emily's face turned crimson, and Hank imagined she must be thinking of twenty-seven ways to roast a younger brother. He enjoyed the situation immensely.

"I don't remember a reference to that particular person, Tim. Should I put him in the story, Emily?" he asked, raising an eyebrow.

Diane met them and, listening, asked, "Will you put me in the story, Hank? I'm the daughter of the house, and we did offer them a home."

"We'll see how it goes," he countered and wondered how the two families and their values could be so different. He turned to Will and Letitia. "Thank you for your hospitality, Mr. and Mrs. Anderson. Diane, I'll be by at seven o'clock next Wednesday night for our trip to the picture show."

He tried to make it sound like a business appointment. His date with Emily, with Tim as their chaperone, was not mentioned.

As Hank left, the group strolled out with him to his car. In the distance, fog had crept in from the bay, and a lonely foghorn sounded, bleak and baritone, cutting through the mist. Drops of moisture fell from a nearby oak.

As the horn drew the attention of the rest, Hank leaned toward Emily and whispered in her ear.

"When I see you Sunday, I'll want to hear all about old Norman."

❧

The church housing the congregation they visited was a square white building with a shingled roof and a tall bell tower. Inside, straight-backed pews faced a redwood podium, and a small loft accommodated the choir Emily meant to join. She smiled at the thought. The church was plain but filled with loving souls who lingered after the service to welcome them.

Leaving the building, Emily and her family felt they had found the body of believers God had led them to join. Empowered by God's Holy Spirit, the pastor's message left no doubt that he had a servant heart. He was a leader whom the Lord would bless. "This seems like a good neighborhood to look for a house, Stanley," said Sarah. "Rent would most likely be reasonable."

Stanley agreed. "Cable cars are available throughout the city, too, so getting to work would be no problem."

Bored with the practical, Tim's mind darted to the treat for the day. "Do you see him, Emily? I don't. He said he'd be here when we got out of church. You don't think he forgot, do you?" He paced back and forth in the grass then did a complete turn in place before giving up to stand cheerlessly beside Emily.

Emily clasped his shoulder. "Don't worry, Tim. A promise is a promise. Hank won't forget."

Behind her, a voice chuckled. "Now that's a vote of confidence if I ever heard one."

"Hank! There you are!" Tim was like a puppy with the fidgets. "We're ready, aren't we, Emily?"

Stanley and Sarah seemed happy to see him. In approving Hank's friendship with her, Emily felt her parents fully expected her to lead him to the Lord.

Hank looked with surprise at the crowd drifting from the building. "Say, a whole bunch of people go to this church, don't they?"

"Yes, and it's a friendly congregation. They certainly reached out to us this morning," said Stanley. "We'll join their membership."

Though her dad reflected happily, Hank appeared ill at ease, and Emily caught her younger brother's hand. "Tim's chomping at the bit, Hank, so I guess we'd better go. Where are you parked?"

"In the back. Why don't you two wait here, and I'll bring the car around."

Tim pulled his hand loose. "Can I go with you, Hank?"

"We'll both go," said Emily. "I'd enjoy the walk after sitting so long. We'll see you later, folks."

Stanley cautioned them to be careful, and he and Sarah started for the cable car stop. Hank glanced back over his shoulder.

"I'm sorry I have only a one-seater. Do you think they'd have accepted a ride in the rumble seat?"

Emily chuckled. "No, and not out of pride, either. They're both fascinated with cable cars. Mother, especially."

"Hey! This is a keen car!" Tim spouted as they approached Hank's black Model-A coupe.

"I washed it so it would look nice for you," he said to Tim but eyed Emily, who tried unsuccessfully to calm a blush.

Speeding along in Hank's little car, the salty sea air off the bay smelled wonderful, and, in the rumble seat, Tim whistled to feel the wind blow the sound away. Emily had brought a scarf for her hair, and after tying it on she enjoyed the ride as much as Tim. She glanced at Hank. He was even more handsome with the wind ruffling his dark hair. It was a wonderful day.

&

Hank surprised them by taking them for a lunch of fresh flounder at a clean, but weather-beaten fish shack near the beach. Hot dogs with chili and onions were on the menu, so Tim was well served, too.

After the delicious meal, Hank took them along the beach road to a spot that overlooked the Seal Rocks. As the frothy green surf roared in, blasting them, hundreds of California sea lions frolicked like children, climbing and feuding, around the sharply pointed rocks. Elated, Tim ran from one viewpoint to another, pointing and laughing.

"This was a nice thing to do for Tim," said Emily. "Thank you, Hank."

He spread his handkerchief on a rock for her, and they sat together. "If you think I did this only for Tim, you're wrong. It was a way to get you out of the house so we could talk. You wouldn't have come if we hadn't brought the little rascal, would you?"

"No, I confess, I wouldn't have. You're not like anyone I've ever met, Hank. You have an overwhelming personality," she said, lowering her gaze, "and you know you're much more sophisticated than I."

Hank chuckled, shaking his head at the frank statement. "And *you* are a very honest girl. Do you realize how rare that is?"

"I'm not being honest today. I can't imagine how Mother and Dad will explain our absence to the rest of the household."

"Why should they have to?" Hank queried, frowning.

"Hank, you have a date with Diane Wednesday night. Have you forgotten? Tim and I haven't dared mention that we would be with you today. It would cause trouble, I'm sure. So you see, I'm not quite as honest as you think."

"The *date* was Diane's idea. Besides, don't you realize everyone's less than honest once in a while? It's nothing."

Emily twisted around to face him. "No, it's wrong."

Hank grinned and looked out to sea. "Is that what you learned in church this morning?"

"Apparently *religion* is a bad word to you. Why?"

"It's okay, I guess, if you need a crutch." Entwining her

fingers with his, he looked down at her. "In my case, I don't."

Emily freed her hand and stood. Hank's conscience bothered him. He'd lied to himself, and now he'd lied to Emily. Of course it was wrong to be less than honest!

Sightseers passed. Emily sat on the running board, and Hank leaned against the fender. Seeing Tim still caught up in the antics of the sea lions, he pushed himself off the car and moved to sit beside her. He couldn't let her think the worst of him. Maybe. . . "I have something to tell you, Emily. The night I came to interview you was not the first time I'd seen you."

"Not. . . When did you see me before?"

Hank recounted the episode at the Arizona bus stop and how he'd almost bought a ticket to San Francisco just so he could find out more about her.

"Trouble was, I had a story to finish. I'd been in the fields with migrant workers, harvesting wheat with a gang, and was about to live with Indians in the desert. I had so much time invested, I had to go on." His eyes pleaded with Emily, "You understand, don't you?"

Excited, she laughed. "I *knew* your face looked familiar. I've been trying to figure it out since the moment you appeared at the house."

"I made you stop and think, huh? Doesn't that suggest anything to you?" His voice lowered, and he ran his knuckle along her cheek. "Quite a coincidence, don't you think?"

Emily didn't believe it was coincidence, but a non-Christian would. She didn't want to lose Hank's friendship, yet the opportunity to tell him about Christ was too open to ignore.

With a gentle touch she took his hand away. "You think it's coincidence and not part of God's plan for our lives?"

Leaning forward, Hank picked up and chucked a pebble

toward the ocean. "What does God have to do with anything? I believe in intelligence and good luck. You've been brought up to believe you *must* obey a higher power, or you'd see that, too."

Unsmiling, she picked up another pebble and handed it to him. "You're a very nice man, Hank Garrett, but you are playing with and dodging the most important thing in life. God sent His Son to die for you. He loves you. He wants you to know Him."

Hank started to argue, but Tim bounced back to point out one sea lion who was sitting on the side of another, and that fat fellow was blaring like the foghorns they heard at night from the bay. No battle resulted, and, finally, Tim lost interest.

The moment was destroyed. Emily knew she could go no further, and soon they were back in the car and on their way to Mission Dolores. *But am I meant to go no further?* she wondered.

five

"The real name of the mission is San Francisco de Asis, but it's more popularly known as Mission Delores," said Hank as they approached the front of the mission. "It was named for Saint Francis of Assisi and constructed of adobe bricks covered with plaster."

"It's got a bell, like our church, Emily!" called Tim, running ahead when he jumped out of the car.

"Look again, Tim. There are three bells, and there's a cross on the roof."

"Wait for us, Tim," Emily ordered. "We'll go in together."

Walking up the stairs, they entered an arched doorway. The sides and the rear wall of the church were made of wood.

"Wooden pegs were used instead of nails as they were in all buildings of that day. The redwood in the ceiling and other locations was tied together with leather. It's a tough old building; not even the 1906 earthquake could demolish it." Hank pointed to the walls. "These interior walls were painted with vegetable dyes. The paint is the original, and the colors are as bright as when it was first built."

"Do you think it would make you sick if you ate any of it?"

"I don't know, but I wouldn't try licking it if I were you." Hank laughed. "Do you remember when the Declaration of Independence was signed, Tim? Don't tell him, Emily!"

"She doesn't have to tell me. It was in 1776!"

"Good for you! Well, five days before it was signed, they held the first mass in this building. But it wasn't officially a

50

mission until October of that year, and the building wasn't finished until 1791."

The three drifted toward the altar. "This is something that impresses me," he said. "Think of all the work that went into hand-carving that altar. See the gold leaf? That was transported from Mexico."

"To be so old, it's beautiful isn't it, Tim?" asked Emily. Tim nodded and when Emily knelt in front of the altar, so did he. They bowed their heads in prayer while Hank stood respectfully to one side.

Afterward, he took them outside to a flower-covered graveyard behind the mission. It was quiet and peaceful. Since it was surrounded by a high wall, part of the city sounds were diminished.

"Some of San Francisco's most famous citizens are buried here. These stones represent Spaniards, Mexicans, Americans, and Indians." He walked ahead, stopped, and waited at one large stone until they caught up. "This is the grave of Luis Antonio Argüello, a native San Franciscan. He was the first governor of California under Mexican rule."

"A big shot, huh?" asked Tim, clasping his hands behind him.

Emily and Hank exchanged smiles at the boy's stance and his attempt at manly conversation.

"Unfortunately, great harm was done to the Native Americans. Foreigners brought diseases that killed more than five thousand people eventually, many from an epidemic of measles. I question whether missionaries should have established missions if they had so little regard for the natives they used to build them."

Not knowing how to answer, Emily tried to diplomatically end the subject. "Hank, I really hate to leave, but I think we'd better. My aunt and uncle may be home by now, and we

don't want to throw their Sunday routine off." She hoped
Hank caught her reasoning.

Time had flown by. As they left the mission and got back
on the road, an orange-gold sun brightened a dark cloud on
its way down, and she wondered if they'd be caught in a
California rainstorm. But the rain held off, and when they got
back to Ingleside Terrace, Emily had Hank let them out at a
car stop. Tim jumped down from the rumble seat, and Hank
came around to open the door for Emily.

"Thank you, Hank," she murmured softly. "It's been a wonderful afternoon. Tim and I have had such a good time." She
sighed. "Now, I have to get back into the house without someone questioning where we've been." Her eyes followed Tim,
who had trotted to the corner to see if the cable car was coming.

"Will you go out with me next Sunday without Tim?" Hank
asked hopefully and touched her arm. "I'll try not to be overwhelming and sophisticated."

Emily giggled and he laughed, too. Then the giggle shut
down, and her voice assumed a beseeching tone. "Would you
come earlier and go to church with us, Hank?"

His face changed, and he took a deep breath. "Emily, I hope
I can make you understand this. I'm not a churchgoer. I think
it's pretty lucky that we've met a second time, and it's not
absurd to think we're meant to be together. But I'd be lying if I
agreed that it's due to some eternal plan. I can't accept religion. There's too much hypocrisy involved. Instead of your
God doing it, I've had to make my way in the world with hard
work and perseverance. I don't believe a person needs anything else."

Trying to control her tears, Emily looked away as he talked.

"Will you come with me next Sunday?" he asked. "We'll
take a drive down the coast. There are many beautiful spots

along the ocean that you haven't seen. Won't you say you'll come?"

Knowing she shouldn't, Emily raised moist eyes to his. She couldn't resist. "Yes, Hank, I'll come with you."

❧

Only their parents were home when Emily came in with Tim.

"Well, there you are," said Stanley, looking up from his paper. "Will and Letitia have been gone since morning, Lee says, *and* they're not expected back until tonight."

With a feeling of relief, Emily looked around. "Where's Clay?"

Sarah, mending a pair of socks, answered. "He's at the Embarcadero. Did you have a good time today?"

"Did we!"

Tim straddled the arm of the chair next to his mother and regaled her with a vivid description of the antics of each sea lion he remembered, then he skipped through the rest of their excursion with Hank. He soon talked himself out.

"Tim," said Sarah, "I'm glad you had fun, but I want you to remember that it might hurt Diane's feelings if she knew you and Emily got to go with Hank before she did. You mustn't say anything at all, Son."

"Okeydokey, Mom. Mum's the word. But she sure is a pill, isn't she?"

Emily nearly laughed, and she saw the effort it cost her mother to keep from smiling. Stanley was deep into the editorial pages of the paper, and Tim picked up the funny pages, so Emily drew her mother away to get over the giggles and chat.

The atmosphere of her parents' blue brocade and dark walnut bedroom invited intimate conversation. Sarah sat on a lounge to listen as she always did when her children had something to share.

"You know me pretty well, don't you, Mother?" Emily asked when she saw her mother poised to hear her dilemma.

"I know when something's bothering you. There's always a clue, like wetting your lips, or smoothing your hair, or touching your throat. You've been doing all three since you got in the house."

Emily kissed her mother's forehead then sat on the edge of the four-poster bed facing her. "Hank isn't a Christian, Mother. He says he has no use for religion, that it's a crutch. My heart hurt when he said that."

"My dear, that statement is as old as the hills. People say it in defense when they think someone may talk to them about Jesus. It's like they're warding off evil spirits." She laughed at the irony, and Emily smiled.

"But," Sarah looked into her daughter's eyes, "if we really care for that person, we don't give up. The Bible says to go out into the highways and hedges to claim those He loves. We have a much better chance to love someone into God's kingdom when that someone *wants* to be with us. Don't you think so?"

"I felt that way, at first. He asked me to go out with him next Sunday, and I was thankful that there might be a chance to talk to him again about the Lord. Then, I asked him to come to church with us, and he told me how he felt about believers. Even though I said yes, I'm not sure I should go."

"We'll pray about it, and God will show you what to do. His will is what you want, isn't it? Even if it doesn't include Hank Garrett?" Emily nodded, and Sarah laid her hand over her daughter's tightly clasped pair. "Emily, you have a special feeling for this man. Why?"

The story of the first meeting came out, and Sarah was amazed. Emily knew how she felt.

"Hank said it was coincidence, but I've had a strange feeling of security since I met him. Could it be that he *is* the one God has for me?"

"How does your heart feel about him?" Sarah reached to smooth a brown curl above Emily's ear.

Emily lowered her gaze. "He took my hand in his once, and I was surprised at how much I wanted him to do that. I realized I'd been waiting for it to happen, and it felt so right."

Sarah breathed a sigh. "You're not a flighty girl, Emily. You're a young woman who has shouldered responsibility. Under your dad's spiritual influence, you've developed into a woman any man should be proud to marry. God's not asleep; if we ask Him, He'll resolve this to His honor and glory. Let's begin."

As her mother prayed, Emily listened, sincerely praising God that there were *two* spiritual leaders in her family.

❧

Arriving at the Embarcadero, Clay had seen Slider right away. He was sitting on a lobster trap near a cook shack. He was dressed the same, cleaner, perhaps, but still identifiable as a worker. Jumping up, he gave Clay an energetic handshake.

"Hey, I've been lookin' fer you! The union boss is back and wants to see you. Be here tomorrow," he said, leading Clay away.

"Sure. What kind of job does he think he can get me?"

"Now, you can't go at him that way, kid. You take off your hat and speak with respect. If he likes you, he'll do something fer you, so you make sure he likes you." Slider looked around and lowered his voice. "He'll want a little money, too. Some cash up front as a sign of good faith."

"I'm satisfied with that. I'll just have to figure out where to get it," said Clay, frowning. He hadn't expected this.

Slider stepped back with a smirk. "Okay, kid, make up your mind. You told me you'd do anything to get a job. Now, you're crawfishin' all over the place. If it's because of the cash you'll be out—forget it! I know lots of guys who'll pay it. I was doin' you a favor. But I guess I'll get somebody who's not such a pantywaist. So long, kid," he muttered and wandered off.

Clay caught up and grabbed his arm. "Wait a minute, Slider. You got me all wrong. Our family's had it rough; money's scarce as hen's teeth. But I'll get the dough someway. Tell me how much to bring, and I'll be here with it tomorrow."

Clay's heart almost stopped when he heard the amount of money he'd have to come up with.

❧

In her room, Emily was reading the contract she'd been asked to sign and return to administration. It was bedtime, and she anticipated a good night's sleep before her first day of school. She jumped at the unexpected rap on her door. "Yes? Come in."

Clay slipped inside. "Did you have a good time with Hank?"

"We both did. I'll let Tim tell you about the sea lions. We ate at the beach then went to the mission. It was a wonderful day. What happened to you?" she asked, wondering why Clay seemed so nervous. "We were expecting you back earlier."

"I met Slider at the Embarcadero and did an errand for him."

Emily didn't like the sound of that. "What sort of errand, Clay?"

"It was kinda strange. All I had to do was drive this guy named Fred Maroni to a nightclub tonight and wait for him to come out. It was a nice place, neon lights all over, set back under some eucalyptus trees. He was in there about an hour, then I drove him back to the house where I'd picked him up."

"Clay, why did you let Slider talk you into driving someone

to a nightclub? You know what goes on in those places. What made you do it?"

"Money."

"Money?"

"Yes, I needed twenty-five dollars, and that's what I get for driving him. I need it to join the union. I can't get the job Slider told me about unless I join."

"What kind of job is it?"

"They haven't told me yet, but I hope it's as a mechanic. Slider told me it might be."

Laying the papers aside, Emily stood, facing Clay. "Now, don't be angry, but be warned. I'm going to say what I think. Why don't we sit down? Here, take my chair, and I'll use the dressing table stool." When they were seated, she started again.

"There's something wrong here, Clay. Common sense tells me no one would give you twenty-five dollars to simply drive him to a nightclub. That's a lot of money."

"Well, I didn't actually get the cash. Slider said it was like credit. They want twenty-five dollars as a sign of good faith to join the union. If I drove Mr. Maroni, he said, it would take the place of my 'good faith' money."

"Did you use his car or someone else's?"

"His, I think. It was brand-new."

"If it was his, why didn't he drive himself?"

"I don't know. Maybe he doesn't know how."

"Clay. . ."

"Well, I don't know. Slider offered, and I saw my chance."

"How did you make contact with the man you drove. . . this Mr. Maroni?"

"Slider took me there on a cable car."

"Did Slider go with you to the nightclub?"

"No, and when we came back he was gone, and I had to pay

my own way home. But I remembered how to get here." Clay scratched his head. "Maybe driving's the job Slider thinks I could get. Yeah! A driver who's also a mechanic. Say, I'll bet that's it!"

"But why would you have to join a union? And pay them first in order to get in?"

"I don't know, Em. I've thought and thought about it. I can't figure it out. All I know is, I'm supposed to meet Slider tomorrow. Mother and Dad are already in bed. I thought if I talked to you, we might make some sense of it."

"I'm glad you didn't talk to the folks. They've got enough on their minds without this." Emily got up and paced the room for several seconds. "Clay, I have an idea. Let's call Hank. Do you still have his number?"

"Sure."

"If he's home, he probably wouldn't mind coming over. As a reporter, I'll bet he's investigated all kinds of situations like this. He could give us good advice. Let's call him."

"Are you sure? Now that I've talked to you, I feel like a fool."

"I may turn out to be the fool, Clay. Come on."

&

Clay told Hank they'd be watching for him, and the two crept out to the street. It was not long before Hank pulled up, and they got in. They decided to drive to the Presidio, the military emplacement, both to show it to Emily and to talk privately on the way. Driving slowly, Hank listened while Clay leaned forward in the rumble seat to relay his story. Then he questioned him.

"Did Slider pay you the twenty-five dollars in cash?"

"No. He said it would be like credit, so I could join the union tomorrow."

They neared the bay. Neither Emily nor Clay spoke. Hank ran his fingers through his hair. Then, as if coming to a decision, he gripped the steering wheel with one hand and turned sideways.

"No, Clay, you're not going to do that. I've been making inquiries, and I have an idea that may benefit both you and your dad. We have some good unions in this town—I belong to one myself—but this evidently is not one of them. Take my word, the twenty-five dollars is a payoff, not an honest union requirement. It's only after you draw a paycheck that dues start."

"A payoff for what?"

"For keeping your mouth shut about where you took Maroni in case you were asked."

"Slider did tell me not to mention it," Clay confessed. "But lots of people go to nightclubs. Why would anyone want to keep it a secret?"

"I'd like to know that myself," Hank replied in a somber voice.

Emily sighed and clinched her hands in fists. "Oh, Clay, I was afraid this meant trouble."

"But I was desperate!" Clay exclaimed. "That's why I agreed to drive the guy."

"If they're in a pinch, desperate men *will* do things they wouldn't do ordinarily. That's what those guys counted on."

Clay frowned. "I told Emily I'd feel like a fool, telling you this."

"I'm glad you did tell me. Maybe I can keep you from *really* being made a fool of, or worse. You sit tight and wait for my call. Don't go near the Embarcadero. Tell your dad to stay where I can reach him, too. What I have in mind may not work out, but if it does, it could mean honorable work for you both."

&

They stopped for coffee at a little cafe on Fulton then went back to the house on the hill. Emily and Clay felt much better. Clay hopped out of the back, said good night, and left Emily alone with Hank.

Clutching her purse, Emily smiled. "Thank you for coming over, Hank. You've taken a big worry off my mind. I knew, coming from you, Clay would listen. He's not dumb. He just needs work."

"I can imagine. These days, it takes more than prayers to get a job."

Emily's eyes filled with tears. "That was ugly, Hank."

She started to get out of the car.

He grabbed her arm. "I'm sorry," he said, pulling her back and wrapping her in his arms. "The last thing I meant to do was hurt your feelings."

His lips found hers in a long kiss. Emily had never been kissed like that, and he did it again. She broke away, at last, realizing she was compounding the problem. She couldn't fall in love with him, not if he didn't believe in God.

As if he knew her thoughts, Hank released her, got out of the car, and came around to her side. He opened her door, and when she stood beside him he spoke to her in a whisper.

"Sometimes it doesn't matter who believes what. It's either there or it isn't. And with us, my beautiful, it is definitely there."

six

Monday morning, Sarah and Stanley enrolled Tim in school in the area close to their church. Several rentals were listed in Sunday's *Chronicle* and they checked on two. Meanwhile, Clay stayed close to the phone in case Hank called.

He didn't call, and since Emily had left early for her first day at Ocean Gardens school, Clay was forced to listen to an hour of Diane's monologue while she waited for her mother. They were invited to a society luncheon for a favored few, she braggod, and Clay resisted the impulse to clap his hands over his ears. Pacing, she gave him a review of their Sunday outing.

"You should have been with us in Sausalito yesterday, Clay. We took the ferry over, of course. That's what we always do. It's so much fun." She smiled slyly and said, "I thought of you stuck in that stuffy old church with those stuffy long-faced people, singing dull old songs." She tossed her beaded bag on an end table and flopped down on the sofa beside him.

"You shouldn't have felt sorry for us, Diane. We met a lot of nice people, and there wasn't a long face in the crowd. In fact, we felt so at home we'll join the church."

"You'll join the church? How much will that cost?"

"Nothing. You know, some things aren't for sale."

"That's not what Daddy says. He says anything's for sale. Anything and anyone."

Her words offended Clay. "I don't believe that. My dad couldn't be bought for any amount. He's been hurt, and he's taken more than a man should have to take, but he keeps his

61

faith in God, and he's true to himself. Dad's tops in my book."

"But he's poor. If we hadn't taken all of you in, you wouldn't even have a place to live."

Snide comments were Diane's trademark, Clay decided, and he'd just have to get used to them. In a way, he felt sorry for her, and he tried to explain.

"You're wrong, Diane," he said. "My dad's not poor. He's rich in wisdom from God."

"Who cares? My daddy's rich in *money*. That's what counts."

Clay got up from the sofa and looked out the front door. An old man carrying a bucket of gardening tools turned the sprinklers on two flower beds he'd finished cultivating. The warm sun made a rainbow of pastel colors in the spray.

"How did Uncle Will make his money, anyway?"

"You know how. He has a big market building downtown."

"But it's just a building with stalls where people bring produce to sell. It doesn't seem like he'd make enough from that to build a fine house and buy all this stuff. He has a big car, too. In fact, the day we came in, there were two cars at the depot. Does he own both of those?"

Diane jumped to her feet. "How should I know?" she retorted, frowning. "What are you getting at, Clay?"

Clay hadn't meant to make her mad. "I guess I owe you an apology. I was getting too personal."

But Diane wouldn't let it rest. "I don't know where Daddy gets so much money. He just *has* it, that's all. I wish people would stop asking me about it."

Diane rushed away almost in tears. Watching her dash to her room, Clay felt confused. As far as he knew, he was the only one who'd asked how her dad got so rich. Why was she mad?

Letitia came in, ready to leave, and she gave Clay a look he had seen often in the past few hours. Keeping the phone covered without explaining why embarrassed him. Clay realized she thought he should be out looking for a job. But they had to do as Hank asked. He hoped she wouldn't convince Uncle Will they were freeloaders.

❧

Wednesday evening, Diane kept the path to the front door busy. Stanley and his family hadn't left for church when Hank arrived, and the long look Hank gave Emily made Diane nervous. She was on her own tonight; her mother and father had gone to an anniversary party. But that suited her. She was in charge. The trick was getting Hank out of the house.

Diane took Hank's arm and edged toward the door. "Let's go. We can see the last of the picture and stay through it again. I love doing that, don't you?"

"We'll go in a minute. I have to talk to Stanley and Clay," he said, shrugging off her hand.

"Oh, all right. I'll wait."

She flounced away, her blond hair swishing. Perched prettily in a chair, she draped her new red dress to flatter her silk-clad legs. But Hank was paying no attention. Evidently he had made appointments for Stanley and Clay to be interviewed by a friend who owned a company.

"Do you mean it, Hank? He really wants to talk to us?" Clay exclaimed through a wide smile.

The speechless Stanley wore a similar look on his face.

"I assured him you were both experienced, and skilled help is all he can afford. If the meeting goes well, you could start tomorrow," Hank said, still casting glances at Emily.

So what was so marvelous about getting a job? If she had to, Diane felt she could get any job she wanted. But there they were, Sarah and Stanley hugging each other, Clay and Emily hugging each other, all of them hugging Hank. Then. . .

What did Hank just do? He kissed Emily's cheek! No one saw but Diane, and she was furious! *She* was going out with Hank tonight. Didn't Emily know that? *Look at them!* Emily was blushing like a bride and smiling at Hank. Well, Diane would show her. Before the night was over, she'd get Hank to kiss *her*. Not a little peck on the cheek, either. It would be a real kiss if she had to do it herself!

"You haven't heard the best part yet," said Hank, still eyeing Emily. "This man has a contract for work involving the Golden Gate Bridge!"

"Oh," said Sarah, her hand covering her mouth, her eyes fearful.

"Don't be scared," Hank assured her. "They can't work on the bridge itself. They'll be doing what they have the skills to do."

"You mean I could work on machines?" Clay's voice boomed.

"That's right. There are a lot of unemployed men in San Francisco, many without specific skills. But my friend needs two or three employees exactly like you. Stanley, you'd be working in payroll. Charlie hinted that, since you know banking, it might be good to train you in all phases of his accounting system. How does that sound?"

"Like the Lord has blessed us again—this time through Hank Garrett," Stanley said as if he could cry.

Hank stopped abruptly then went on. "I'd like to explain something. I told Sarah you two couldn't work on the bridge, and this is the reason. To be fair to the state's unemployed, a law was passed that anyone hired to work on the Golden Gate Bridge must be a resident of the state for one year.

"You see, hundreds of people have moved to California for jobs, but people here are having a hard time, too, and they're being robbed of honest labor. Dozens of men show up at the bridge every day hoping that, if a man gets hurt, they'll have a chance at his job."

Emily and Sarah gasped, and, though it was true, Hank seemed to regret saying it out loud.

"Let's get back to your case. Stanley and Clay will both be working for Charlie's company. Clay will do work for Charlie's regular customers, releasing another of his men to maintain machines they built for use on the bridge. It's a new company, but, since getting the bridge contract, he expects his company to grow despite the hard times we're going through. There's a chance for a good future for both of you."

Enough was enough! Tired of congratulations and tears, Diane stomped to Hank's side to break up their happy little party. Not that she wouldn't be glad to see Stanley's family leave, but they didn't have the jobs yet, and she and Hank were going to be late to the picture show.

"If you're through getting jobs for everyone, Hank, isn't it time you took me to the show, like you promised?" she asked with a stingy smile.

Hank agreed and, with a last look at Emily, reminded the men of their appointment time. Plans for her good-night kiss percolated in Diane's mind.

❧

As soon as Diane and Hank left for the movie house, Stanley's family boarded a cable car for church, utterly happy. God had used Hank to give them an exceptional gift. Tomorrow, dressed in work clothes just in case, Stanley and Clay would report for interviews at the machine company belonging to Hank's friend.

Following prayer meeting, the pastor told the Andersons he had heard of a house for rent not far from the church.

"It isn't a big place, but it has three bedrooms and is in good repair," he said, confident the Andersons would want it.

"We're very grateful, pastor. If we get the jobs, I'll call you as soon as possible," said Stanley.

"Good! Then I'll let the owner know, and he'll arrange to let you see the house."

The men shook hands, and on the ride home, Emily reveled in her parents' happiness. Her father's expression had lost its hangdog look; he was basking in the first ray of hope for a brighter future. Her mother, overjoyed to see her husband so happy, encouraged him every mile of the way. *A marriage made in heaven,* Emily thought. She prayed that she, Clay, and Tim would have Christian homes like the one God had blessed their parents with.

Will and Letitia, too, were overjoyed. "Well, that's wonderful, Stanley," said Will, smiling widely. "This is a big break, and I know how happy you must be!"

Letitia was equally solicitous. "Oh, yes! We know how anxious you must be about getting a place of *your own!*"

Emily wondered if they were really glad for them or elated with the prospect of having their home to themselves again.

On the sly, Lee let Stanley's family know he was happy for them by laying out a splendid repast of sandwiches and tea in the dining room. Through their friendship with the man, Emily had discovered a secret about the imperturbable Chinese. When his mistress complained too much, he ignored the edict of economy and did as he pleased. On this night, both families retired having eaten well.

❧

Diane had managed to capture Hank's hand in the theater at once, and she never let go. Her next move was to lean her head against his shoulder. Hank felt as trapped as an animal in a zoo.

"Wouldn't you like a bag of popcorn?" he whispered.

"No, it's too messy. Besides, I don't want you to miss any of the picture."

"I don't mind."

"Thank you, but I couldn't eat a thing. I have to watch my figure, you know."

He sat back, and Diane snuggled closer. Hank thought of Emily's family. How happy they were! Charlie Hogan was a friend from his University of California days in Los Angeles. He had run into Charlie last Saturday at the Golden Gate site. Hank had been there to finish a story. They'd recalled old times, then in serious conversation, Charlie had mentioned that he was in need of three skilled workers.

Stanley and Clay had experience identical to two of the slots he had open, and Charlie promised to give Hank a call. He'd kept his word, so Hank had little doubt they'd be hired.

Emily's expression tonight was all he needed to know he was falling in love with her. Her joy reached out to him, and he had found his lips on her cheek as the family had hugged him. But he wanted much more of her than a kiss on the cheek.

Glancing down at Diane, he tried without success to extricate his hand. She simply smiled and ground more face powder into his suit coat. Promising himself never again to be trapped by the little schemer, he waited patiently for both pictures to end. Then, he left the theater as fast as he could pull Diane away from the playbills of coming attractions. He couldn't wait to be rid of her.

"Wasn't that marvelous?" she trilled as he dragged her along. "I could watch Bette Davis forever. Do you think we look alike?"

"I'm afraid I hadn't noticed."

"We both have light hair. I don't like long brown hair. It's so ordinary. But I do like black. It makes me want to run my fingers through it."

If she makes a move toward my head, I'll smack her, Hank told himself. Fortunately, they reached the car before he had to make good his mental threat, and he handed her in.

"This has been one of the best nights of my life. Imagine me on a date with the famous Hank Garrett. Do you know what an honor that is?" She laid a hand on his arm.

Hank left her to get in the car. "I'm just a newshound, Diane, nothing more. Now, it's late, and as soon as I get you home, I'm shoving off. I have to get up early in the morning."

"Oh, Hank! I was in hopes you'd take me to get a sandwich."

"I really can't tonight, Diane. And, remember! You have to watch your figure."

He started the motor, and Diane sulked all the way home. It was the first break he'd had since they started out. But as he pulled the car to a stop in front of her house, she threw her herself at him, wrapping her arms around his neck.

"You've been wanting to kiss me all night, haven't you? Well. . .so have I." Diane pulled his head down and pressed her full lips to his.

This girl is an octopus, thought Hank as he tried to loosen her hold.

❧

Emily had bathed, spent time in prayer, and read her Bible. Her first classes at Ocean Gardens had gone well. No child seemed to be a problem. Maybe when the children got used to her, one or two would cause trouble, but, so far, they were all well-mannered and cooperative.

She turned off the light. The full moon shone into her

window, and she rose from the bed to view it. The city lights shone far away, but the moon shed a far more romantic light on the flower beds and lawn. It was still; not even a dog barked. With San Francisco's many fogs, it was a longed-for night.

She started to turn away when she noticed a car below on the driveway. Pulling the curtain aside, she peered out. Hank and Diane were sitting in his car, kissing. Not only were they kissing, but to Emily, they seemed to struggle to get closer.

At that moment, Hank pulled away and looked directly at her window where the moon shone on her white-clad figure. His upturned gaze stayed for a long moment, holding her still. Finally, tears streaming down her face, Emily turned from the window and threw herself on her bed.

≈

"Are you thad, Mith Andathen?" Polly Blair lisped, holding Emily's hand in both of hers.

Emily smiled and hugged Polly. "Of course not, dear. The wind blew a piece of dirt in my eye. You go on now."

"Okay!" Her Shirley Temple curls bouncing, the little blond smiled and ran off to play with her friends during recess.

It wasn't true. Emily was sad. Though she'd had a long night to mull over what she'd seen between Hank and Diane, she hadn't been able to throw it off as she'd prayed to do. She liked Hank more than she'd thought. Or was it love?

Logically, she had no reason to expect Hank to choose her over Diane. Diane was pretty, she had lovely clothes, and she was rich. She wasn't a Christian, but neither was Hank. Emily hadn't thought of that. Would Hank turn to Diane because she placed no spiritual limitations on him?

But life in Christ was not restricted as Hank thought. It was freedom. She wanted him to see Jesus as she saw Him: her Savior, her Best Friend, closer to her than any human on Earth.

She couldn't imagine life without the Lord. Yet that's where Hank was, and so was Diane. Without Christ. It was the saddest thought of all.

&

Emily left school that afternoon eager to learn the outcome of the men's job interviews. Hank again. Hank had cared enough to use his influence to get their appointments. Even if they lost out on the jobs, it didn't take away from the concern he had shown. How could she *not* like the man?

Sarah and Tim met her at the car stop. Smiles wreathed both faces, so Emily knew it was good news. She jumped down and rushed into their arms. Viewing the family's exhibition of joy, passengers smiled and chuckled as the car swooped away.

"Is it absolutely certain?" Emily asked, almost afraid to believe good times were possible.

"Yes! Stanley used the office phone to tell me they'd both been hired, and he sounded *so* happy. Oh, Emily. . ." Tears crept down Sarah's cheeks as they hugged again.

"And guess what?" shouted Tim, not to be outdone by the men of the family, "I got a hundred on my spelling test!"

"Timmy," Emily sang, "you're a hero, too!" She cuddled him, kissing him till he wiggled to get away.

On the walk to the house, Sarah told Emily the only details she knew. "Yes, they both have jobs. The pay is small, but paychecks will be coming in at last, and each one has a job he likes. As Hank said, Stanley will be in accounting, working with numbers again. He's a genius at that, you know," Sarah said as a matter of fact. "And Clay will repair and maintain his beloved engines and machinery." She laughed.

Emily could hardly wait to hear the rest when the men got home. Hank might be gone, but they were a Christian family, and God had taken care of them. In the Bible, Matthew 6:33

said, "But seek ye first the kingdom of God, and His righteousness; and all these things shall be added unto you." That promise from the Lord was all that mattered. It mattered much more than Diane and Hank being together.

seven

With his intermittent, unique smile, and without telling Letitia, Lee put together a fantastic dinner. Will and Letitia were a bit critical of the obvious cost at first, but they relaxed as the meal was served, and it ended up being the happiest evening Emily's family had spent in Will's home.

Only Diane was obdurate. Tight-lipped and glaring, she refused to let go of her warped view of the visiting family.

To Emily she spoke with brittle sarcasm. "You think you're okay now. But I bet you'll be back, begging Daddy for a handout. Your family's poor, and you'll always be poor unless somebody helps you."

What had she to gain by such sullen remarks? Emily was embarrassed for her. Her psychology teacher would have said Diane felt threatened and wished to relegate them to a lower status than her own.

But Emily did not hold grudges. When they moved, she hoped Will's family would visit them often. The renewed kinship between the brothers was too dear to let an eighteen-year-old girl's cunning nullify it. *All families have to make allowances,* she thought.

For dessert, Lee served ice cream sundaes topped with whipped cream and maraschino cherries. The doorbell rang as they began the lavish treat, and Diane jumped from her chair to answer. A voice Emily dreaded to hear replied to Diane's greeting in the living room. Emily wished for an escape. Her body rigid with tension, she prayed God would show her how to act.

Diane came in laughing; Hank was silent.

Rushing to him, Clay held out his hand. "I don't know how to thank you, Hank. You're the best friend a guy ever had."

Stanley smiled, nodding as he shook hands. "That goes for me, too, Hank. Our whole family thanks you."

Emily kept her seat while the rest rose in welcome. Her mother glanced at her oddly but said nothing. When conversation returned to normal, Emily listened as the day's events were retold. Her eyes had still not met Hank's.

Unhappy out of the spotlight, Diane seized their attention. "If you're through congratulating yourselves, I'll have Lee bring Hank some ice cream."

Letitia clasped her hands at her bosom. "Oh, dear! I must apologize for being less thoughtful than my sweet daughter. Lee, bring our guest some dessert," she said, and she and Will rearranged the chairs to make room for Hank.

Not knowing she was doing Emily a favor, Letitia seated Hank far down the table on the same side. Emily said little, and conversation went on without her.

An hour later they left the table, Diane clinging to Hank's arm. Emily stayed in the living room long enough to realize Hank had no plans to speak to her—not that it was the time or place, and not that she wanted him to. She would leave word at the *Chronicle* that she would be unable to meet him Sunday.

When she finished holding a skein of yarn her mother had wound into a ball, she rose from a stool beside her. "If you'll excuse me, I have to prepare a special project for my students." At the stairs she turned and smiled. "Good night, everyone."

Hank made as if to rise, but Diane grabbed his arm and whispered in his ear. He turned to her with a dumbfounded look, and Emily escaped.

ॐ

Sunday, after church, the family looked at the house their pastor had suggested, and the owner brought the key. It was smaller than their Kansas home, but the rent was reasonable, and it was a place they all liked. The cottage was on a cable car line. With five cents and free transfers, they could be at work, school, and church in minimal time.

They had no furniture, but they had been tightfisted with their Kansas money, and Emily and Sarah were expert bargain hunters. First, they needed good beds. Sarah refused to buy used mattresses. Part of the outlay, then, went for new ones, though they had no bedsteads.

The family went over each night that week to clean the windows, floors, and walls of their new home. The plan was to move the following weekend. Emily found the return to normalcy welcome, and she delighted to see her family so happy.

At church on Wednesday night, the members learned that the men had secured the jobs they had prayed for. Answered prayer was always a happy moment for the church family. Later, one of the ladies came to Sarah and Emily with a question. "We're wondering if you'd be open to some help we can offer. We know you have to replace all the furniture you had to sell in Kansas. We don't have money to help buy new things, but several of us have pieces of furniture you could refinish if you don't mind the elbow grease it would take to redo them."

Sarah's eyes twinkled. "Why, Greta, we'd be grateful! Wouldn't we, Emily?"

Emily smiled at the short, rawboned woman. "Absolutely! Refinishing furniture is one of our favorite pastimes. Mother and I have spent hours at it. Refinishing is one job that gives back more than the effort you put out."

"That settles it, then! We'll find a way to get the things over to you as soon as we can," said Greta, changing arms with her Bible. "Emily, I guess school is going well?"

With her affirmative answer Emily gave the lady a little hug and more thanks for her help.

a

Settling into their house was achieved by degrees. Clay and Stanley came home tired at night, so deferring some of the heavy jobs, like carrying in a secondhand stove and icebox, meant days of eating sandwiches. In the meantime, the mattresses were delivered. Letitia had given them five bed pillows from her linen closet surplus, so the family slept well.

Another of Letitia's contributions was a small gateleg table she had retired. With the addition of furniture by the church members, several orange crates, and bricks and planks stacked to create bookshelves, the house began to look less vacant.

"Furniture donations make us look like poor relations to some people," Clay laughed. "But I don't mind. Do you, Emily?"

"Not at all. Most of the church things the owners could have refinished themselves. I think they were just being kind. Besides, we're all moved in now, and we'll soon have this place looking like our own home. You wait and see."

The two had finished a cold Sunday-night supper. Sitting on the back steps of the house, resting from a hard day's work, they watched the sun move toward the west. Stanley, Sarah, and Tim had gone to take back the car Stanley had borrowed from his brother.

Clay made note of the vehicle. "Do you remember the extra car Uncle Will brought to the bus depot to get us?"

"Wasn't it the same car he loaned us today?"

"I think it was, and I—"

"Anybody home?" Hank Garrett called, coming around the corner of the house. "I knew you wouldn't leave the front door open unless someone was here."

His sudden appearance caught Emily off guard. She couldn't leave; she was immobilized. And she had yet to thank him for what he had done for the men. She owed him that courtesy, at least. He had literally changed all their lives—not just hers. The gray pants and gray plaid coat he wore were striking. Broad shoulders did the coat no harm either; he was handsomely built. His shirt was crisp and white, and he was wearing a tie. Yet he looked tired. She probably did, too. At present, though, fatigue wasn't the reason she was having trouble breathing.

Clay jumped up in welcome. "Long time, no see, Hank."

He was making the situation worse. Normally, Emily would have at least hinted to Clay that she suspected an attachment between Diane and Hank, but she hadn't. She couldn't bring herself to tell anyone about the kiss she'd seen. It was too painful to recall.

"Had to run down to L.A. for a week or so." Closing the distance, he placed a hand on the railing. "And how are you, Miss Emily Anderson?" he asked, a tremble in his voice.

Did he have to look at her that way when she was wearing the old slacks and blouse she'd worked in? She forced herself to answer.

"I'm fine, Hank. A place to call your own is as good as they say."

"I'll bet." He moved to drop down beside her on the steps while Clay sat cross-legged in the grass facing them. Hank pulled his gaze from Emily. "Where's everybody else?"

Clay pushed back a front lock of hair. "The folks went to Uncle Will's to take back a car we borrowed today. Emily and I were discussing it, and I was about to add something. I haven't said it out loud because it seemed so far-fetched, but I *think* I saw the same car parked next to the nightclub I drove Maroni to that night. Uncle Will has never said the extra car belongs to him, but it's always there when he wants it."

Hank's eyes narrowed as he listened. "I wish you'd search your memory for any detail that would pin that down, Clay."

"Why?"

"I can't say right now. Think. Was there a distinguishing mark on the car like a cracked window or—"

"That's it! I knew something rang a bell. I noticed a piece broken out of the taillight as we left the depot, but I didn't think anything of it. There's lots of those around. But at the nightclub I saw it again. I didn't notice the taillight today, and I wouldn't have remembered at all if you hadn't made me dig for it just now. Is it important?"

"It could be." Hank seemed unwilling to say more.

With a cunning smile Clay got to his feet. "Think I'll go meet the folks and Tim at the car stop. Bye!"

He was up and gone before Emily could shift her mind in gear to stop him. She was alone with Hank.

"Emily," he started, "like it or not, we're going to talk about it."

"You don't owe me an explanation. I was in the wrong place at the wrong time. I shouldn't have watched; it was none of my business."

Hank turned and grabbed her shoulders. "How can you say it's none of your business? Don't you feel anything for me?"

Emily lowered her head rather than answer. Hank's arms left her shoulders. "So that's it. You've crossed me off because

I don't go to church."

"You're wrong, Hank. I'm not that judgmental."

"Then don't judge me until you hear me out." Emily looked up and nodded. "You deserted me the night the date was set up," he said. "Remember?"

"I told you why. You overwhelmed me."

He smiled. "And later on, *you* overwhelmed *me*."

Her face burning, the memory of their kiss swept over her again. "Then why did you kiss her?"

"Who?"

"Hank!"

"Do I make my point? It meant nothing. Emily, it was a put-up job. I couldn't get away from her! She kissed me, not the other way around. You have to believe me."

Emily clasped her hands and leaned forward, arms between her knees. "I have quirks in my character, Hank. One is that I can never again trust people who have lied to me. As long as you remember that, I'm ready to be friends."

She sat up and held out her hand to shake his. Hank looked at her hand and again into her eyes, grinning. He took her hand, shook it, and with a little jerk, pulled her to him. His kiss sent the same thrill shimmering through her. But it didn't last long enough.

"Emily! Emily!" Tim's thunderous footfalls rang through the near-empty house. "We're back! Hi, Hank!" The screen door slammed behind him. "Clay said you were here. Are you going to take us somewhere?"

Again, Emily felt her face warm. "He doesn't have to take you out every time he comes to see us, Tim."

Hank chimed in, "It's a good idea. Want to see the bridge?"

"You mean the Golden Gate Bridge where Dad and Clay work?"

"Yep."

"Could we, Emily? Could we?"

She had a mountain of work to do for her children at school, but the light would soon be gone, so they would be back home in an hour or so.

"Where would we go? Not to the site, surely," she said.

"No, we'll go up on Telegraph Hill. I know a spot where you can get a swell view of what's going on."

❧

It was true; Hank knew the perfect spot to view the bridge. He, Emily, and Tim piled out of the little roadster to look. The bridge had taken form, but there was a collection of cranes, exposed cables and steel, catwalks, and machines on its surface. It was a mammoth project. They wandered to a spot where pink and white oleanders bloomed, and a section of stonework lent a perfect viewpoint. Tim crawled up on a guardrail to sit.

"This is a miracle in the making," Hank said. "The Golden Gate Bridge will be the largest suspension bridge ever built. None was ever built at a harbor entrance, either. That's because the winds constantly shift, and tidal undercurrents are powerful. Add to that the violent storms and blinding fogs, and you begin to see the dangers these men have confronted to build it."

"Then why are they trying to put it there?" said Tim.

Hank swept his arm in that direction. "Look for yourself. Have you ever seen anything so magnificent? If all goes well, 1937 will see it finished." He lowered his head beside Tim's and pointed. "Tim, when the two half spans are connected, the bridge will be cambered. That means it will go up in the center and down toward those two towers. The middle section is 4,200 feet long. And see how the cables sag down over the center? That's why it's called a suspension bridge. It's all suspended from the cables hung over the two towers at each end."

"How can cables be strong enough to hold it up? I never saw a cable big as that," said Tim.

"The idea came from a German by the name of John Roebling. He invented a spinning machine that spins steel wires together into a giant wire. Then, they apply a massive amount of pressure to thousands of those wires, and they squeeze them together to make the cables. The cables on the bridge are a yard wide, Tim."

"Wow!" the boy exclaimed.

Emily had a question, too. "Hank, what is that filmy thing under the bridge? The wind's waving it a little."

"That's a net that Mr. Strauss had made. Remember? The bridge was the dream of Joseph B. Strauss. He didn't want such a beautiful structure to be remembered for the tragedies that could happen during construction. He had four nets, woven out of half-inch manila rope, hung under the bridge to catch anyone who might fall. The net extends ten feet beyond the sides of the bridge, and it's moved as the bridge progresses. It was an expensive safety precaution, but it's already saved lives."

"It seems so dangerous even with the net," said Emily.

"It's very risky. Safety is drummed into the men's heads every day. Workers wear hard safety hats. It doesn't apply to Clay's job, but all companies with men under contract to work on the bridge must follow strict safety regulations.

"Drinking or pulling stunts is cause for being fired on the spot. In fact, they're experimenting to find diets to cure dizziness and hangovers, and some of the men wear glare-free goggles. They'll try any idea that will cut down accidents.

I've talked to enough workers to feel the close camaraderie between them. They trust each other. They have to; bridge men never forget where they are."

Emily let out a breath. "I'm glad of that."

"How do you know so much about it, Hank?" Still perched on the rail, Tim sat totally engrossed in the account.

"Research on stories for the paper. It's my job to know what's going on in San Francisco."

Emily felt proud. She'd read all of Hank's articles and stories, and he had outstanding talent.

A dusky freighter moved out toward the strait, and the three watched as its wake through the blue waves increased with speed.

Tim turned back to Hank. "Are you going to write a book someday?"

Emily smiled; that had been her next question.

"I'd like to," Hank answered, "but I intend to see some of the world first. There are places I've wanted to go all my life, and it takes more money than I've got right now."

"You'll get there, Hank," said Emily. "I know you will." But her heart was breaking.

The schoolteacher from Kansas wanted a home and children with a Christian husband. In one moment Hank had demonstrated how little he fulfilled that dream. He wanted nothing to do with the Lord, and he couldn't travel the world with a wife and children tagging along. A sense of loss crept stealthily over her.

Why hadn't she looked at facts instead of letting emotions carry her away? Hank Garrett had never been a romantic possibility for her. For Diane, maybe, but not her. If she didn't want her heart to break further, she'd have to be more cautious. *Jesus, help me,* she pleaded silently. *I can't do this by myself.*

Hank took her hand. "Come on, Tim. Let's get back to the car. We have to get your sister home to grade papers or whatever she has to do."

At the black coupe, Tim climbed into the rumble seat. "Do you think the bridge will really be done next year, so we can cross it?"

"They're building as fast as possible. I've heard it will be ready by summer. That may be an exaggeration, though."

"What's an 'exaggeration'?"

"It's a tale that sounds better than it is."

Like the one I've been telling myself, thought Emily.

Hank squeezed her hand and closed the door. She'd have to get over him, that was all. She'd have to learn to be his friend and nothing more. But she still yearned to introduce Hank to her Savior. She wanted him to have life at its best, and the best could be found only in Jesus Christ.

eight

Back at the house, they were getting out of the roadster as another small car pulled in behind them. Diane, wearing violet slacks and a checked shirt, jumped out and ran to meet them.

"What do you think?" she asked, motioning to the blue car she'd parked. "It's mine! Daddy bought it for my birthday. It's not until next month, but he knew how much I wanted one, so I got it now. Isn't it smart? Want to go for a ride?"

Tim had no trouble deciding. "I do!"

"Not this time, Tim," said Emily. "Tomorrow's a school day." She smiled at Diane. "It is for me, too, Diane. Thanks, anyway. Maybe we can go later."

"That's okay. Hank and I don't mind." She stepped close to him. "You drive, Hank." She handed him the key. "There's a little noise in the motor. Maybe you can tell what it is."

Dismissed, Emily started up the walk.

"Not tonight, Diane, I have to talk to Clay," Hank said, backing away. "I'll tell Clay you need his help. He's the mechanic in the family. 'Night."

Watching Tim amble up the walk backwards, Hank fell in step with Emily. She winced at the slam of the blue car door. Hank didn't look back, but Emily knew he was leaving behind a very angry girl.

❧

Emily and Hank saw each other nearly every week, but there was no outward change in their relationship. Emily stayed

83

out of Hank's reach, though the love she felt for him was growing. About his feelings she refused to guess.

When the men were home and Tim was around, general conversation ended, and talk of the great bridge began. But when Hank came, and because of the stories he wrote, he contributed facts about the bridge the others didn't know.

"I see they're painting the structure again to protect it against the elements," said Stanley, settling in his easy chair.

Clay, sitting with Hank in donated chairs, chortled at a memory. "Right after we got here, I saw a guy painting in a bosun's chair, hanging from a girder, whistling as if he hadn't a care in the world, and he was over two hundred feet above the water."

"Clay!" said Sarah, entering the living room after finishing supper dishes, "I think you save those stories just to scare the daylights out of your mother. Did you really see that?"

Grinning, he leaned forward. "I give you my word, Mom."

"Oh, dear!" Sarah sighed. "No wonder folks get hurt."

Hank spoke to reassure her. "I've told Emily and Tim how strict the safety rules are. There have been injuries, yes, but believe me, everyone is safety-conscious. The accident rate is less than normal. I've talked to engineers who claim there's usually a death for every million dollars spent on a bridge. But that's a theory, not a fact. Mr. Strauss is determined that it will *not* be true on the Golden Gate." His smile went past Sarah.

Emily came in, returning his smile, and sat on the wicker love seat beside her mother. From a basket she picked up a hoop holding a pillowcase she was embroidering.

"If I hadn't seen the work progressing and the potential beauty of the bridge, I'd be wondering whether it was worth the risk," she said. "But now, there's no question."

"It will be beautiful, Emily," said Stanley. "I've seen the

artist's drawing. San Francisco will be proud of herself."

"She is already," Hank said, moving to sit on the floor by Emily. "The thirty-five million dollar bond issue passed by a huge margin. That isn't to say there weren't political stands and arguments pro and con about the practicality of the bridge."

Hank glanced cautiously at Sarah. "Delaying tactics were used in the beginning in an attempt to scuttle the project. For instance, it was argued that if there was war and the bridge was bombed, naval ships couldn't get in or out of the bay. The bridge would block the strait."

"Wow!" said Tim, whom Hank and Emily had taken to the harbor to see returning navy vessels, including a battle-ship. "I hadn't thought of that." Tim sat with crossed legs facing them.

Hank ruffled Tim's hair, as usual. "Don't worry about it, sprout. Nobody's going to bomb us *or* the bridge."

"Speaking of worrying," said Emily, "who is this Adolf Hitler who's taken power in Germany? Is he someone the United States should worry about or not?"

Hank looked surprised; although he knew he shouldn't be. Emily was an intelligent, inquisitive lady.

He played the whole thing down for Sarah's sake. "I think Hitler's making a lot of noise, so far. Maybe he's just mad at Jesse Owens for the big hit he made at the Olympics." He laughed.

૪

On October 16, 1936, prayers of praise were offered by Emily and her family for a man none of them knew. He jumped aside and fell, unhurt, into the bridge net when a piece of heavy equipment on rails hurtled toward him. Stanley put the accident into the proper perspective, praying it would bring the man's family closer to the Lord.

Not so fortunate was another worker who, within the week, fell into the net. The net was not taut, and he fell to the ground on the north, Marin County, side. His spine was fractured. The Anderson family's prayers changed to petitions for God's healing, both for the accident victim and those he loved, who stood vigil at the hospital.

Following those accidents came a worse one. On the bridge on October 21, a pin in a crane pulled loose, and the huge machine collapsed on a worker. That man died, but another was saved from death. A cable whipped out from the falling crane and knocked the second man into the net, and he was uninjured.

Stanley and Clay came home immediately after the accident, surprising Sarah. Then, while they had coffee at the kitchen table, Stanley explained to her, and later to Emily, the reason they had come home early.

"When there's a death," said Stanley, "it's a matter of ethics for workers on the bridge to go home for the day, and Charlie Hogan honors that tradition. Clay and I only slightly knew the man who died. Still, the news was hard to hear."

"That's because you value God-given life so highly, Dad," said Emily, wanting desperately to comfort him.

Sarah clasped the hands of both Stanley and Clay. "God wants us to care about those around us. Right now, those workers have families that need prayer, and that's what we must do."

They were on their knees, talking to the Lord, when Hank appeared at the screen door.

Stanley heard his movement. "Come in, Hank," he said, standing up to let him inside. "We were praying for the families of the men who were killed and injured."

"I don't want to interrupt. . . ."

"We'd love to have you with us, Hank," said Emily, standing. "We don't always pray on our knees, but this seemed to be a time when we should."

Inviting Hank to a chair, the family took seats and continued their prayers.

৯

Years had passed since Hank had been in a prayer situation, but he had never before experienced a breathless space of time in which God seemed so real. To Hank, God was a word, not this living presence the Andersons made him feel with their prayers. As each prayed, it was almost like a conversation, and that with a beloved Friend.

Not even Tim was self-conscious. His prayer was so simple and straightforward, it made Hank wonder if he'd had *any* understanding of spiritual matters at Tim's age. In fact, he had no religious standards as an adult to compare with this boy of eight years.

There were smiles all around when they finished. Had God really comforted them in the aftermath of a tragedy? Hank had to wonder. The evening went on as usual; he had coffee and cake with the Andersons, but their prayers had disoriented him. He had actually partaken of the quiet peace that permeated their home, and it was frustrating not to know why it was different than other homes. His own, for example.

Not that I need religion, he chided himself mentally. It was a matter of logic. Most people lived in the real world as he did. He often saw something on the order of these tragedies. Emily's family didn't. If they lived in an atmosphere where crime and cruelty and bloodshed were common, they wouldn't pray either. Of course they wouldn't.

৯

The monitors collected the children's permission slips, and

Emily finished taking roll, checking the slips against it. One of the monitors took the slips to the office. When she returned, Emily lined the children up and hustled them into the hall. Betty Amos came out of the room opposite Emily's.

"What a morning!" gasped the third-grade teacher. Her roll and permission slips dropped to the floor, and Emily stooped to help pick them up. "Isn't that just like me? Finally get to make a field trip, and I'm trembling so I can't make my fingers work. I 'spose the second grade's ready," she said forlornly.

"Yes, we'll meet them out by the bus."

"Oh, I'm the last one!" She signaled her class to come out.

Betty reminded Emily of her friend, Velma Hawley, in Kansas. Like Velma, Betty was older, yet she looked to Emily, as Velma had, for the confidence she lacked.

Emily smiled, remembering the letter her mother had received from their next-door neighbor, Mrs. Flemming, in Brewster. The letter notified them they had shipped the last of the Andersons' boxes, which had been stored in the Flemmings' attic. Their boxes would arrive COD at their permanent California address.

Almost as an afterthought, Mrs. Flemming had mentioned that Velma and Norman Conner were seen together socially quite often. What a relief! Let Hank tease her about "old Norman" now. Emily almost giggled. She had always suspected Velma's inquiries about Norman were more wishful than she wanted Emily to guess.

Betty and Emily lined up and marched their students outside. Joining the second grade, the chattering children climbed aboard, and the teachers counted heads. Taking her seat, Emily was glad she'd worn a lightweight suit; it was a warm day.

"How many parents volunteered to chaperone for you,

Betty?" Emily called, over the bus noise and children's voices.

"Two, in the black Dodge sedan. How about yours?"

"Two also. No fathers. It's a workday. My Mrs. Fall is a good driver, and their car is in good shape. It's the second-grade chaperone I'm afraid won't make it. Her old car needs a lot of prayer." Emily chuckled lightly.

The children rode in boisterous excitement until they arrived at the San Francisco Public Library. Noisy as they were on the bus, the sight of the awe-inspiring library had a sudden quieting effect.

The children and their chaperones moved through the huge marble entrance hall and climbed the august marble staircase. Emily's class, overcome by the vastness of the building, inched closer to their teacher. Knowing the trip was a big step for them, Emily softly encouraged the first graders to be bold.

Three guides joined them, and the groups were separated for their tours. Emily's guide directed the curiosity of her group to a display of wall murals depicting California's history, and helping out, Emily described and explained features in the murals with simple words the children could easily understand.

Less interesting to the students, but important to Emily, was a collection of manuscripts and first editions of works by California writers. Thinking of their interests in common, she determined she'd ask Hank to come back with her at a later date to inspect and discuss them. She wondered if he knew some of the writers and could tell her more of the background of the works.

The assistant guiding the little ones through the library took the children into every department she thought they could comprehend.

Finally, Emily stopped in a hallway and quietly talked to her class. "Girls and boys, this library, this big building, was built especially for all of you. It's here to help you to read more and to find out about the world around you.

"In the books you've seen, you can find out how children in other countries live. You can find out what kinds of foods they eat, what they wear, and the music they like. The books tell you about things you want to know."

"Will they tell you how to sail a boat?" one boy asked.

"I'm sure there are many books about boats, Keith."

"Is there a liberry book about ducks, Miss Anderson?"

"There are lots of them. Ask your mother to come to the public library, and you'll be able to take a book about ducks home with you. You and your parents can enjoy it together. Our trip today is to show you what a nice building this is, and how nice and helpful the people are who work here, and how many beautiful books are here for you to enjoy all your lives. Think of that!"

To Emily, the excitement in the children's voices was reward enough for the effort spent to make the trip.

The last area they visited was the music department. A piano was available for the public to try out musical selections in the library collection. Tired by now, the children stirred restlessly, and only the few who were taking music lessons acted interested. But Emily knew what would energize them.

She adjusted the piano stool to play. "Let's see who can tell me what this song is!" she announced.

Recognizing the melody, the children's faces brightened, and they began to call out names of other tunes. Emily played all their requests for popular songs. To develop their appreciation of classical music, she chose light, gaily written tunes by Mozart, Prokofiev, and Richard Wagner. The children clustered enthusiastically around the piano and clapped after every piece.

Joining them for the last part of Emily's little concert, children in the other two groups clamored for more. She played *Jesus Loves Me,* and the youngsters' response was so energetic the library guides quieted them, laughing. But it was time to leave, and reminded of a promised snack at school, the children happily departed and boarded the bus in a mood of celebration.

The bus began to move, and Emily called out. "Driver! Wait! One of our chaperone's car isn't starting."

The man stopped the bus. "You want me to go see if I can help?"

"Would you?"

He hopped out, trotted to the car, and, after taking a look under the hood, led two frustrated women back to the bus.

"They'll have to ride back with us. Their distributor cap is cracked."

"My brother is a mechanic," said Emily to the chaperone. "He can probably help you get a new one and fix it for less than someone else would charge." The woman smiled her appreciation.

By letting three children sit in two of the seats, they made room for the extra passengers. The women climbed on board, took the seat behind Betty and Emily, and the bus got under way. "I thought it went well, didn't you?" asked Betty, and the rest agreed. "Maybe now they'll let us have more field trips. You're the one we have to thank, Emily. Until you came, the outings we put before the board were never approved."

Emily thought she knew the real reason. "Don't give me undue credit. Like others, our school has gone through bad times. Maybe this was God's time, *plus,* the trip was the answer to a lot of prayers."

"You're right, Emily. Even the board has to go along when God decides the children need something a little extra."

⁂

"This is going to be the craziest Christmas we've ever had," Tim complained. "Where's the snow?"

"In California, you have to go to the mountains for that, Son." Stanley laughed. "But look at your tree. I don't think we've ever had a prettier one. Emily and your mother did a lot of work, stringing those cranberries and popcorn. The walnuts covered with tinfoil look like real Christmas balls, don't they?" Stanley's eyes traveled upward. "And look at the star on top. Wonder where Emily got the gold tinfoil to cover it?"

"No telling. I guess all that stuff's okay, and red paper chains make it look good, but I hope we can get some more lights next year. Eight lights is not very many."

"I know," Stanley sympathized. "But lots of kids don't have electricity, much less lights." Stanley stopped for a moment. "Son, you're not forgetting the real reason for Christmas, are you?"

"No, Dad. I know Jesus is the reason we have Christmas. Friday is the day we'll celebrate His birthday this year."

"When we get to church on Christmas Eve, I'm sure the pastor will read from Luke's Gospel about Christ's birth. I never get enough of that Scripture."

"Do you think Hank would go with us if we asked him?" Tim's expression looked serious. "I'd like for him to hear the pastor tell about Jesus. Then, maybe he'd believe in Him like we do. Emily would sure like it. She prays for him every day."

"We all do, Son. Don't you?"

"Well. . .not every day, but I pray for him."

"Good for you, Tim. Never give up."

"Never give up what, Dad?" asked Emily, coming through the dining room from the kitchen.

Tim bounced from his chair to preview the plates of fudge and divinity she carried. Behind her, in the dining room, Sarah set a bowl of fruit and nuts on the table Letitia had given them and turned off the light. Smoothing her brown hair, she came to sit in her rocker beside Stanley's easy chair.

"To answer your question, Emily, we were talking about Hank's salvation. Tim and I agreed we will never give up praying for him to find Christ."

"Thank you, Dad, and you, too, Tim. It will soon be the New Year, and I can't think of anything I want more from 1937. Hank is such a fine man, but he claims he wants nothing to do with religion," she said, heaving a sad sigh. "He doesn't know what he's missing, and I don't seem to be able to convince him."

Sarah groaned and clapped her hands. "What's going on here? Stop this dismal talk! Hank Garrett *will* be saved. Let's put our faith to work and expect it!"

Ashamed she hadn't also exhibited a positive attitude before Tim, Emily hugged her mother. Then, she grabbed another morsel of candy and stuffed it in Tim's mouth and took one for herself.

Sarah reached for candy, too. "So, do you think Hank will have Christmas dinner with us?"

"I hope so," Emily said between bites. "He's not going to L.A., and Clay and I have both invited him. If he's not on an assignment, I think he'll be here. So will Celia Grant. I made a special trip to the board of education office to invite her, although I'd asked her to come the last time we had lunch together."

"I'll be glad to meet and thank her, at last. You wouldn't have the job at Ocean Gardens if it weren't for Celia."

"She's a wonderful Christian, Mother. You'll love her."

"Where's Clay tonight, Sarah?" asked Stanley, leaning over for his second piece of divinity.

"He had a date, of all things. I thought he was never going to find a girl out here."

Stanley laughed. "When you're nineteen, Sarah, there's always a girl."

nine

Christmas morning dawned bright and cloudless, but cold for California. The family opened gifts early because Tim awakened early. Though modest, their gifts were carefully chosen with the receiver's hints in mind, and everyone was happy.

Preparations for the turkey dinner began immediately. Some of the food, noodles, candied yams, salad greens, sweet rolls, and pies had been prepared the day before and stored in the icebox. Except for the pies and salad, the rest of the food was now warming on top of the oven. Waiting to be finished were pots of vegetables on surface burners as the turkey and dressing baked in the oven.

They would eat buffet style from the kitchen as the family could not yet afford a dining table with matching chairs.

Sarah refused to settle for less. "Until next year," she declared, "when everyone can be seated at a table accommodating several guests, we'll eat *buffet!*" Her family was not surprised.

Celia Grant arrived at eleven o'clock with a bouquet of red hothouse flowers for Sarah.

"Oh, Celia, all we've wanted was to meet you, and you show up with beautiful flowers that must have cost a fortune!"

Emily saw the gathering mist in her mother's eyes and knew how pleased she felt.

Clay was even more pleased. Emily had mentioned Celia many times, but, until that day, he had not set eyes on her. Her red-haired beauty was a conspicuous surprise. Emily

95

squelched a smile at Clay's dumbstruck expression. Obviously enraptured with her creamy complexion, wide brown eyes, and freckle-sprinkled nose, he stumbled over every other word he uttered.

Letitia had sent their regrets when invited, so they were not waiting for Will's family and they could begin their dinner. But as of one o'clock, Hank, in spite of multiple invitations, had not arrived. Emily's expression betrayed her pretense at gaiety.

Stanley called for a circle of prayer around the table. He thanked the Lord for His holy day, His blessings to each of them, and for the food He had provided. Then, with gusto, they helped themselves to the delicious feast, prepared by Sarah and Emily.

"Let's take our plates and eat on the back steps, Celia," Clay suggested, his tongue-tied state past. "It's warm outside, now." Hearing the couple joke and gab, Sarah whispered to Emily, "Listen to those two, would you? Celia has a sense of humor as good as Clay's. Could be he's met his match at last!"

Shave and a haircut raps at the front door brought Stanley to his feet. He set his plate down, peeked out the window, and turned to a hopeful Emily.

"Looks like the reporter got here after all!" He opened the door. "Come in, Hank, come in! You're just in time to help us get rid of the turkey!"

"We were afraid you'd been called away," Emily said, meeting Hank and waiting for his welcome to subside. Her eyes drank in his tall posture. "Come fill your plate."

"Lead me to it," he said, eyeing Emily's royal blue dress trimmed with lace. "You're looking pretty tasty, yourself."

"Thank you, but you don't have to sing for your supper, you know. We'll feed you even if you come up with nary a compliment."

"And who gave you sassy pills, today, Miss Emily Anderson?" he asked, his eyes glowing with warmth.

"I feel wonderful! It's a beautiful day, we're all well and employed, Clay and my friend, Celia, like each other, dinner is delicious, and you're here."

Hank's face sobered. "Does my presence make you happy?"

"Of course, it does, Hank." Then she caught herself and forced a wide smile. "So does Celia's."

❧

I wonder where that leaves me, thought Hank. He'd never even toyed with the idea of settling down until he met Emily. Since then, his urge to see the world had also cooled. She and her family were struggling, living on a strict budget, but they were happy. As his eyes rested on her and the beautiful dress she wore, he guessed it had taken careful planning to afford both it and the festive dinner.

She didn't know his complete story. She didn't know that his family was as rich as hers was poor, or that he chose to live on his salary alone and not on family money that belonged to him. If she knew why he did it, she wouldn't like it.

In Los Angeles, he had spoken to his family about Emily, and while his parents were pleased to learn Emily was a Christian, his sister, Frances, was not impressed. A tall, sturdily built brunette, she displayed a learned attitude of pessimism.

"I suppose this means you'll be spouting Bible verses and saying prayers all the time," she had said when they were alone in the expansive library of their Beverly Hills home.

He'd answered curtly, "Emily isn't like that, Frances. Neither is her family. There's a warmer atmosphere in that little home of theirs than ever existed in this big, extravagant mausoleum where we grew up."

"You mean you don't feel the holy nature of God flowing from these walls?" Frances had laughed. "Why Hank, the ladies of the church gather here each Thursday to sew for the poor—and tear every absent member of their heavenly group to shreds."

Hank had paced up and down, forgetting the coffee Frances had poured from a silver server. "Why do you think I moved out? I couldn't take any more of our parents' hypocrisy. Dragging us to church every Sunday, all our lives, yet never giving of themselves—just money. And did Christian principles ever enter in? How many mortgages has Dad foreclosed on to get property with a high resale potential? Some people might think our parents have changed since their *spiritual renewal* this fall, but I'm not one of them."

"I intend to get out. I'm tired of their scrutiny," said Frances. "I'm looking for a reasonable male with all his faculties, and when I find him I'll marry and never return."

There their conversation had ended, but Hank had given it a good deal of thought, since. What *was* the difference between Emily's religion and that of his parents'? The Garretts' spirituality had only one rule—church attendance was mandatory. The rest of the week was up to the individual, but there was no family Bible reading or prayer. Left on his own, Hank hadn't bothered, either.

With Emily's family, their faith was their life, the exact opposite of the Garretts' as far as he could see. The Andersons were single-minded, too. No divisions. They were welded together by their belief in God.

Emily should have been disgusted with him; he had thrown her beliefs in her face more than once. Like the lady she was, though, she had never reproached him. Was it because of her godly principles or simply her refusal to take offense? She had that kind of nature. He was curious; which was it?

❧

"I'd like to go someplace, Celia, wouldn't you?"

Dinner eaten and the leftovers put away, the family and their guests relaxed and chatted over coffee in the living room. Tim stopped examining the Christmas tree ornaments to listen.

"Nothing's open, Clay. It's Christmas," Celia returned.

"I know a place that's open," cut in Hank.

Six interested faces turned at once. "Where?" they asked in chorus.

"Chinatown."

"Oh, Clay! Wouldn't that be fun?" said Celia, her green eyes shining.

"Could I go? Please?" Tim begged.

Stanley shot up out of his chair. "Let's all go! Hank, leave your car here, and we'll catch a cable car. We're all free for once, and Emily told us before she got to California that Chinatown was one place she wanted to go."

❧

Jabbering and laughing, the group hopped a car at the stop, and, jackets in hand against a cool evening, they found seats together. The conductor was a chubby man whose red Santa hat set a holiday mood for his few passengers.

"Why don't we sing 'Jingle Bells'?" asked Emily.

"Good idea!" Hank replied, and he started off without them.

Tim caught up, and the rest joined in. The song triggered cooperation of other passengers, and as if it were a festive sleigh ride, they sped along, clanging at intersections, defying the warm day.

Celia cast a dimpled grin at Clay. "That was good! Emily sings soprano, Hank sings bass, and you sing awful."

"Watch out," he threatened. "Little girls get spanked when they talk naughty!"

"I haven't been spanked since I went to grade school."

"Did it happen often?"

"Once." Celia raised her chin and looked out the window.

Emily enjoyed the exchange, and, from his expression, so did Hank.

Clay wasn't diverted. "May one dare ask what this rare punishment was for? Or would that be embarrassing?"

"That would be embarrassing."

Clay persisted. "Tell us, Miss Grant, or we *won't* go to Chinatown."

Sitting behind with his parents, Tim, who thought there was real danger, leaned forward. "Tell him, Celia. I want to go."

"Oh well, Tim, if *you* want to know, I guess there's no way out." Half turning, she bit her lip and squinted. "I was about your age, and I kicked a boy in my class. He told on me."

"Why did you kick him?" asked Tim, all attention.

Celia blushed. "Because he tried to kiss me, and I wasn't about to let him. And, Tim, don't you ever do that."

With a wry face, Tim declared, "Who, me? I wouldn't kiss an old girl."

"Neither would I," said Clay, smiling. "Anytime Celia wants me to kiss her, she'll have to talk me into it."

"Hope you don't get tired waiting," she answered with a withering look.

Clay's face reddened, and the others chortled at her saucy reply.

≈

Walking down Grant Avenue in Chinatown, Emily felt she was entering another world.

Women they met dressed much as they would have in China. Costumes ranged from drab to ostentatious. A worker wore dark trousers and shirts with white stockings and tiny black heelless shoes or clogs. At the other end of the scale, slender, brightly colored silk dresses, decorated with gold or silver, outfitted women with sleek black hair entwined with shiny ornaments. Emily wondered if some had made wrong choices for their lives.

Men dressed either in western business suits or a variety of black or blue matching coats and trousers. A white jacket with dark trousers denoted a servant of Lee's caliber.

Color was the primary enchantment. Shops were jammed with thousands of unique, crowd-pleasing articles, from cooking vessels to exquisite ceramics and jade jewelry. In one shop, ebony screens set with striking mother-of-pearl designs fascinated the three women. One screen of uncommon beauty caught Emily's eye, and she was surprised when Hank spoke up behind her.

"I'd be happy to buy that screen for you, Emily. Won't you let me?"

"I couldn't, Hank. It's too expensive, and it would be out of place in our little house. Don't get me wrong; I appreciate your wanting to, but no."

"You should have beautiful things around you. Look at this shelf of treasures," he said, pointing to a display nearby. He picked up a stunning vase. "Do you like this?" Emily nodded, breathless at the jewellike enamel colors in relief. "Please, let me buy it for you for Christmas." Meeting her eyes, Hank said, "I wanted to buy you a gift, but nothing was beautiful enough until this."

Her gaze lowered. "What a nice thing to say."

Emily's answer was meant to cool the intensity building

between them. His offer to buy her a beautiful present made it hard to keep her feelings for him out of her eyes, but she *had* to treat him only as a friend. She looked away to quiet her pounding heart.

"Emily, don't act as if I'm some stranger. I want. . ."

"You shouldn't feel obligated to buy me anything, Hank. We're the ones who owe you."

They had walked away from the others, who were inspecting a display of decorated eggs in ornate brass holders. Ignoring Emily's comment, Hank asked the Chinese lady for a box as he paid for the vase, and, nodding with a tiny smile, she brought it back wrapped in bright tissue paper. His gaze tender, he handed it to Emily.

"Thank you, Hank, so much," Emily said, at a loss to show gratitude and still exit a perilous mood. She led the way outside. "Look at the kites and banners decorating the street." Wondering what Hank would have said he wanted for Christmas, she kept her voice light. "The colors are so vibrant. Chinatown is unique, with its upturned roof corners, the children playing with their puppets and toys in front of the shops, and look—look at those three old men, arguing, smoking their long pipes. Grandfathers are grandfathers all over the world, aren't they?"

"Avoiding the issue won't make it go away," Hank said. "We have deep feelings for each other."

Emily couldn't dodge his gaze. "I don't—"

"What's next?" Clay called, dragging Celia from the shop with Stanley, Sarah, and Tim close behind.

"Doesn't anyone else have the slightest desire for a cup of hot tea?" asked Sarah. "This *is* Chinatown, isn't it?"

Stanley laughed and stepped farther out into the street to allow his view to sweep the buildings left and right. He pointed.

"There! There, about a block down. Here we go."

The little group took off, Tim complaining he didn't like hot tea, and Emily promising he could order another beverage.

ᕅ

Once inside the teahouse, they found a large round table, covered with a spotless white cloth, that would accommodate them all. It was watched over by a Chinese man with the same inscrutable countenance as Lee. Emily kept expecting their sly old friend to pop out of the kitchen at any minute.

While the rest drank tea, Tim enjoyed a sweet rice drink. Clay called attention to a large red circle on the wall on which the menu was printed in gold.

"Get this! Bird's nest soup—what do you suppose it could be?"

Hank grinned but said nothing.

Stanley adjusted his glasses and, narrowing his eyes, looked for an explanation but found none.

"Well, the price is certainly right. Let's all try a bowl."

Emily's enthusiasm led the rest. "Yes, yes! New foods are fascinating. What a good idea, Dad!"

The soup was served, appetizing and nutritious in its "bird's nest" of glassy noodles lining the bowls.

"Boy, Dad! This is good stuff!" Tim exclaimed, his spoon scooping the soup again and again.

To Emily the day was a day of magic. Partaking of another country's culture on Christmas day was a treasure, and, she silently conceded, so was Hank's nearness.

ᕅ

Tired but happy, carrying her precious box containing the vase from Hank, Emily, with the family and their guests climbed on a cable car and rode home, conversing in hushed voices.

The evening grew cool as expected, and the house had a

welcoming warmth when they entered it. Sarah set out left-over turkey and sweet rolls, added stalks of celery, and Emily made a pot of coffee. Along with dessert, the group savored happy memories of their trip.

Emily thought gratefully how special their celebration of the Lord's birthday had been. In her prayers that night, she asked again that Hank's heart be opened to the Lord. As much as she cared, their happiness together was slipping away with his failure to acknowledge his lost condition.

❧

"I don't see why everyone gets to go out on New Year's Eve but me," wailed Tim, throwing his leg over the arm of his dad's easy chair.

"Not everyone goes out, Tim. Your dad and I are going to stay home and listen to the celebrations on the radio." With the small radio still a novelty, Sarah easily dissuaded him.

Emily ruffled his hair as she'd seen Hank do. "Don't envy me tonight, Tim. Hank is looking for a line on a story, and I'm tagging along. My school was *very* impressed by the article he did on the family. I want to see what he does this time."

"That sounds exciting! I'd like to—wow!" Tim jumped up, looking toward the bedroom he shared with Clay. "Do you look snazzy!"

Standing unruffled in the doorway, Clay sported his blue, three-piece, pin-striped suit with a starched white shirt and a dark blue tie. His black wing tips shone, and he carried a black fedora.

Polishing his fingernails on his lapel, he asked, "Okay?"

"Okay? Clay, you look elegant. Where are you going? As if I didn't know," Emily teased, smiling her pride.

"Celia and I are having a late supper with her folks, then

we're going to her church for a New Year's Eve watch service."

"You'll have the Grants in awe," said Emily. "If that's what you're after," she added with a puckish grin.

"I wish you didn't have to go to another church for a New Year's Eve watch service. Next year, maybe we could suggest that our church have a watch-night party. Our young people could invite their friends, and nobody would get in trouble."

Laughing, Clay hugged Sarah and kissed her hair. "I promise I won't get in trouble. I'll keep an eye on Celia, too. You know how she is," he said, rolling his eyes and grinning. He waved and headed for the door. "Gotta go!"

Having taken back his chair, Stanley was looking over his paper, smiling and shaking his head. Sarah closed the door behind Clay and turned to Emily.

"It's a foggy night. Be sure to take a warm coat, and do tell Hank to drive carefully."

ten

"Does it bother you to drive in such a terrible fog?"

With the car's canvas top up, Hank and Emily were creeping along, watching for oncoming cars. The roadster was equipped with fog lights, but not all vehicles were.

"Don't worry, Emily. I'm used to it. Are you warm enough?"

"Yes."

"You aren't very talkative."

"I'm trying to be observant," she said. "How do you go about finding an idea for a story?"

"By being observant."

They laughed, and Hank reached for her hand and held it. "Tonight, we'll be observant together. Your beautiful blue eyes will be a big help."

A speech so flattering cautioned Emily. So far, she had kept their relationship on an even keel, and she intended it to continue that way. Since they'd had a phone installed, Diane had called twice, both times inquiring about Hank's visits. Emily had mentioned the calls to him and had given him Diane's telephone number as her cousin requested, but she didn't know if Hank had talked with her. At present, however, he evidently had other things on his mind.

"Emily, remember Mr. Maroni?"

"Yes. The man Clay drove to the nightclub that night."

Hank nodded. "I've discovered Maroni is part owner of that nightclub, but I haven't learned who the other partner is."

"Why? Is it important?"

"It may be. I think something fishy is going on, and I intend to find out what it is. Maroni is in on the nightclub, and I'm wondering if he's connected with the problems on the docks. Is he one of the rabble-rousers, or is he too smart for that? Unions are getting attention these days because of reports about Communism. If not a union, what *is* he mixed up in?

"Also, Clay was supposed to cough up twenty-five dollars before Slider could 'put in a good word for him.' I wonder how much money lines the pockets of those who solicit for unions that don't play by the rules? I also wonder where the buck stops. Men are desperate for work. Clay was desperate for work. A desperate, unemployed man can be steered in the wrong direction—from workman to party member." He let out a long sigh. "You see, I've got plenty of theories but no answers."

"But you do believe you're on to something."

"You're right. Think about this. Clay could earn his initiation into the union by doing a *favor*—Maroni needed a chauffeur. But I think he was being set up for more than that. Driving Maroni permanently would have involved Clay. I suspect it would have led to other, shadier 'favors.' If Maroni is connected with something crooked, Clay could never divulge what he knew about Maroni's activities without making himself suspect. Maroni could have held that over Clay's head forever."

Emily shuddered at the thought. "Thank you so much for getting him away from them, Hank." She wondered now if they were really after a feature story. "You're not looking for a new story, are you? You're looking for more evidence to back up what you already have."

Hank kept his eyes on the road. "Want me to take you home?"

"No. I'm not scared," she said. "Where are we going now?"

Hank laughed and caught her hand again. "What a woman!"

They drove several miles, then Hank turned the car off the main thoroughfare onto a narrow blacktop road. Ahead, a colored blur in the fog turned out to be neon lights. At the end of the road was a nightclub.

"This is where Clay brought Maroni, and where he thought he saw your uncle's car." Hank drove slowly around the building.

"I don't see the connection, though. Uncle Will could have had business here. Our family doesn't frequent nightclubs, but maybe he does. He did go out at night while we were staying there."

"Evidently I've called it wrong. You'd have recognized the car by now if it were here. Let's go back."

Emily wondered: Would Hank have stayed longer, had she not been along? It wasn't like him to leave a story. She'd read enough of his work to know he was like a bulldog, not letting go until he was satisfied. Pleasant as their time together had been, Emily had a strange feeling about tonight. Hank Garrett was on the trail of someone who would definitely wish he wasn't.

After stopping at a block party and eating hot dogs to celebrate the New Year at midnight, Hank took Emily home. At the porch of the house, he started to kiss her.

"Hank, please come to church with us Sunday," she murmured.

His hands dropped from her shoulders to his sides. "Emily, stop hounding me about going to church, will you?"

Emily felt as if he'd struck her. "I'm sorry, Hank, I—"

"Forget it. Good night." He gave her a peck on the cheek.

❧

Diane had watched Hank come out of the *Chronicle* building

every day for a week. She knew the exact time he left unless he was on an assignment. She had followed him in her little car at a safe distance when he *was* on an assignment: to the Golden Gate Bridge site, to the Embarcadero, and once, to a little nightclub where she had trouble parking her car where it wouldn't be seen. The reason for that trip she couldn't imagine. Hank didn't drink. Yet he stayed at the club for almost an hour.

There was another place he frequented that she couldn't explain. Stanley Anderson's little dump of a house. His car was there a lot. It was probably to see Clay. It couldn't possibly be to see Emily. Nevertheless, she had seen them leave together more than once. Why did he continue to see her? What could they have in common?

Emily was a colorless little nobody who had no skill at being a woman. Emily might be four years older, but Diane knew she was twice the woman Emily could ever be. Diane was ready for marriage. She had dreamed about a man like Hank Garrett all her life, and now she'd found him. No one was going to stand in her way. Especially not cousin Emily Anderson. She had to get Hank alone, so he could find out how fascinating she was.

If Hank came out at his normal time, she would make him talk with her, and, if they talked long enough, the battle would be won. She sat back, thinking of the arguments she would use to convince him they were meant for each other. It shouldn't be difficult. She already had a head start.

When she met Hank, she'd come up with a shrewd idea. She'd had him investigated. Her daddy gave her a generous allowance each week; by saving it and pawning gifts she didn't like, she accumulated the cash. She checked the classifieds and hired a private detective from San Francisco's low-rent district.

Her naïve mama and daddy wouldn't think she was capable of such a thing, but they were wrong. She'd done it. The man she hired laughed when he told her how easy the job was. Hank Garrett was from one of the richest, best-known families in Los Angeles. The only son. The heir. Yes, he had a sister, but Diane didn't see her as a problem.

It was surprising that Hank lived only on his salary. That wouldn't keep her in silk stockings. But she'd use her influence once they were married. All that money was there to be used if she gave Hank a logical reason for getting into it. She knew how to handle men. She handled her daddy and the boys she went with, and she could handle Hank, too.

She snapped to attention as Hank hurried out of the building and headed for his car. Opening her door, she got out fast.

"Hank! Hank!" she called, running down the sidewalk toward him. He didn't hear her at first, and, despite her high heels, she had to run faster. "Hank! Hank Garrett!"

He turned and smiled when he saw who it was. Score one. That smile put her miles ahead. Catching up, her hand pressed to her chest, she stood panting before him.

"What's the rush, Diane? You on your way to a fire?" he asked, grinning.

"No," she gasped, "I was trying to get your attention. I need help." Diane took a few seconds to get her breath. "My car won't start," she said, at last. "I was hoping to get a ride with you."

"Where is your car? Maybe I could take a look at it."

"Oh, it's a mile down the next block, Hank. If you'll give me a ride now, I'll have Daddy send a wrecker for it."

She could see him thinking it over. "I don't have anything to do right now," he said. "I'll be glad to take you home."

"You're a darling." She smiled and pointed ahead. "Isn't that your car?"

"Yeah, let's go."

Hank opened the door of his roadster and waited while Diane lowered herself provocatively into the passenger seat. He loped around to the other side and got in.

"I haven't had a thing to eat for hours, Hank. This has been a crazy afternoon. I'm supposed to go to a party tonight, but I'm so upset after having car trouble I couldn't possibly. Can't we just go to some quiet little restaurant, have supper, and talk over coffee? My treat."

It's a brilliant plan, she thought. He was probably out of money 'til his next paycheck.

"I guess I have to eat sometime," he said bleakly. "It might as well be now. Where did you want to go?"

"I know a little place down on the bay. Take the next right, and I'll show you how to get there."

❧

The restaurant was made to order. High-backed booths lined one wall of the seaside building. They took one of those instead of a table. Diane couldn't have chosen a better place or time. It was quiet, the supper was good, and they did talk a long time while he had coffee.

She made him admit, first, that he came from money. He told her about his sister, whom he said he loved, and about his parents, with whom he said he didn't get along.

"I'm glad you told me, Hank. Now you won't think it's terrible of me when I say I don't care for my parents either."

"But your parents adore you. Don't forget, I've seen you together."

"They act like they're *my* children. They do everything I tell them to do. They're silly."

"Diane. . . ," he said with a critical look.

She had to be careful or she'd go too far. She wanted his sympathy, not his contempt.

Smiling, she began again. "Do you know what I'm looking forward to more than anything?"

"I can't imagine. You have everything you want."

"No, I haven't."

"What, then?"

She was back on the right track now. "All my life, I've wanted just one thing. I've wanted to find a man I could love, marry him, and make him the happiest husband in the world."

"Well, you're a pretty girl, Diane. That shouldn't be hard to accomplish."

Diane reached for his hand. "I knew you'd understand. That's what you want, too, isn't it? I mean, you want to marry the right girl."

"Sure. Someday."

"Could it be me, Hank?"

"What?"

His inattention frustrated Diane. She was losing him. She had to get down to business and make some headway! Her fingers traveled over his.

"I said, could the lady you're looking for be me? We have a lot in common, Hank. We've both had a social background, and I happen to know you're quite a man about town. Emily doesn't know that, does she? We both have wealthy parents, and we like the things money can buy, like a nifty car and nice clothes. The only thing Emily has is her stupid religion." She raised his hand to her cheek. "We'd be much better for each other, Hank. Don't you see?"

"She's hung up on religion, all right," Hank admitted as if it really irked him.

"That's why we're so right for each other," she said. "We don't let a crazy obsession clutter up our thinking. We're not weak like Emily and her family. We believe in ourselves." Her eyes locked on his. "Don't you see, Hank? I'm the girl for you, not Emily. I would never mention God, and with me, you'd never have to go to church, or that *prayer meeting* they have. Religion would never come up."

Pulling back his hand, he motioned for the waitress. "I think we'd both better go home and think this over. Your idea may look different to you in the morning, and I'm afraid you'll regret some of the things you've said."

She was wrong about his being out of money. He insisted on paying the bill, and he still had money in his billfold. The newspaper business must pay better than she thought.

They left the restaurant, and when they were back on the road there was little conversation. Diane convinced herself he was mulling over the points she'd brought up. He'd look at her differently from now on.

ও.

After leaving Diane at home with a kiss she'd planted on him "for your trouble," Hank thought about what else she'd said. Diane wasn't Emily, not by a long shot. Like the sophisticated women he was used to, though, she knew how to get what she wanted. In a way, it was flattering.

He'd been so locked in on Emily he'd forgotten he was usually the pursued, not the pursuer. Lately, Emily seemed to be dancing around him, not letting him get close. At UCLA he could have dated a different girl every night. Guys used to razz him about women lining up for him to ask them out.

Diane was right about something else, too. This religion thing was giving him a headache. If he forgot Emily and dated Diane or one of the girls at the paper a couple of times, he might break the hammerlock Emily had on him.

He could always backtrack if he didn't like it. But would Emily still be there? It worked both ways. He'd seen men ogle her when they were out together, and he didn't like it.

When she was with him, she never gave them a glance. Only he had her attention. And when she looked at him with those enormous blue eyes. . .

He shook his head. If he intended to analyze this thing, he had to stick to it. Religion—that was their problem. Emily rarely mentioned Jesus Christ to him, but His name came up in the family's conversations. It came up when they prayed, too. Why were they always praying? You'd think the world couldn't turn unless the Andersons prayed about it.

That's how they were. Even Tim. That little kid wanted him to be a *Christian.* He didn't know beans from apple butter, but Hank could tell from things he said that he wanted Hank to accept Jesus Christ as his Savior. Tim had done it two years before. Was that supposed to make him feel like a sinner because, in almost thirty years, Hank had not?

Diane was right. He should get out more. Look the field over. He'd been thinking Emily was the only one who mattered, but, in a city the size of San Francisco, there were hundreds of girls. She wasn't the only one with gorgeous blue eyes. Those others wouldn't always be reading the Bible, either.

He parked his car and climbed the outside stairs to the back of his apartment house. So why wasn't he happy? He'd made a good decision, one he should have made a long time ago. On the landing halfway up the stairs, he stopped, leaned on the rail, and looked out over the sparkling city lights. Thinking about getting back into circulation should be giving him a kick. Why wasn't it?

ka

"Don't you think this was a good idea?" asked Celia. She took sandwiches, fruit, and a thermos of lemonade from the lunch basket and set them on a checkered tablecloth on the grass.

"I always think food is a good idea," Clay said, grabbing a sandwich.

"Aren't you going to say grace?"

Contrite, Clay thanked God for their food. Then, eating sandwiches and drinking lemonade, they watched the Sunday afternoon crowd picnicking and taking advantage of the beauty of Golden Gate Park. The park contained over a thousand acres; in the distance was the Pacific Ocean.

"You're familiar with the park," said Clay. "What should we see when we're finished?"

"First, the Natural History Museum and Stow Lake. Oh! And one of the windmills. There are two, on the northwest and southwest corners of the park. Then, we'll mosey over to the bandstand for the concert. It's always good. The bandstand is in that direction," she said, pointing, "and, last, the Japanese Tea Garden."

"I can see I've missed a lot, not having a tour guide until Christmas," said Clay, thinking how pretty Celia looked, so dainty in her little brown dress and her hat with daisies on it.

"Ah, but when you did get one, you got the best. Don't you agree?" she asked, peeking at him through lowered lashes.

Clay wanted to kiss her. Who would have thought when Emily brought Celia to Christmas dinner that he would find her above every girl he had ever dated? He thought of her every day. He could be greasing a torn-down engine, and into his mind would pop a brown-eyed girl with flame-colored hair. He had prayed God would lead him to the one he would marry, and it was Celia.

"I'm sure I couldn't have found a nicer guide in all San Francisco," he said, enveloping her with his eyes.

"What's this? A sincere answer? I expected you to laugh. I was being a coquette," she said, fluttering her eyelashes. "Now, tell me," she leaned back against a tree trunk and bit into a ripe apple. "Do you think Emily and Hank are in love?"

"I have my own ideas, but she hasn't shared much with me."

"Or me. I think they love each other. But Emily will never marry him, Clay. Not until he lets Jesus into his heart. She's one of the strongest Christians I know."

"It could be God is testing them. He's testing Emily for sure. And who knows? Maybe He's testing Hank, too. When I think how the Lord let me bring them together in California after they had seen each other at a bus stop in Arizona, I'd say it was His plan all along. Hank may struggle, but if he's meant for Emily, that's the way it will be."

The look Celia gave him reflected his affection for her.

They finished eating and toured the park as planned. The municipal band drew a crowd to the bandstand, and Celia and Clay sat on the grass to listen. By the time they got to the Japanese Tea Garden, they were ready for a cup of tea.

Rice cakes and tea were sold in little thatched teahouses by dark-eyed Japanese girls, dressed in native costumes of floral prints. Though they were attractive and polite, to Clay none had Celia's appeal. Once he'd seen her, no other girl came close.

After their tea, they strolled across a graceful arched bridge to a meticulously cared for garden. They paused at a granite shrine and knelt beside it. Thinking of it as an altar to God, they held hands and breathed a Christian prayer.

"Isn't it wonderful that God hears us regardless of where we are?" asked Celia as they walked away. "San Francisco is a melting pot of so many nationalities, and Christ loves them all. Since we met, we've experienced two foreign cultures together, and here we've had prayer to our living God."

Clay smiled down at a face that reminded him of sunshine, and he spent the rest of the afternoon pretending Celia was his wife.

eleven

Clay's face was pasty white. Tears ran down his cheeks, and he stared with haunted eyes. Sarah ran to him and led him to a chair. He was trembling as if he had a chill.

"Clay, what is it, Son? Is it Stanley? Has something happened to Stanley?" she demanded, shaking his arm.

His tormented expression wounded her. He shook his head but didn't speak.

Sarah put her arms around him. "It's all right, Clay. Take your time. I can wait."

For minutes, Clay cried, trembling, holding onto his mother like a little boy frightened by a nightmare. Whispering soothing words, Sarah stroked his back and waited.

Finally, he burst out, "It was terrible, Mama! I can't stand to think about it!" he rasped, almost crushing Sarah in his frightened grip.

"Take your time, Son. Real slow and easy." Sarah's nerves were burning through her skin.

"They fell, Mom," he sobbed. "They're gone. No one could do a thing. They had to let them go without a chance to survive. Why, Mom? Why did God let them fall?"

Sarah let out the breath she had been holding. At least she knew a little of what had happened. There had been a fall. But what else? How bad was it? Was Stanley safe? Until he came, she feared she would know nothing; Clay needed no more pressure. From his muttering, she gleaned the fact that all work on the bridge had shut down. That meant Stanley would be home, too.

When Clay would let go of her, she helped him to the kitchen and gave him a cup of coffee. His clothes were grimy with grease and dirt. She got his shirt off and washed him, satisfying herself that he was uninjured.

Now, Clay was absolutely silent. Sarah had never waited so long for life-or-death information. And her wait was not over. *If only Stanley would come,* she thought. Was Clay wrong about him? Was he all right? Why hadn't he come home with Clay?

Before Clay could come out with the story, Hank arrived, bringing Stanley and Emily. All three wore stunned expressions. Clay, still shaking, turned his head to hide his tears.

"Has he told you, Mother?" asked Emily in a quiet voice.

"Only a little," said Sarah. "I still can't make out what happened."

"There was a terrible accident on the bridge," Emily explained. "Ten men are dead."

Covering his eyes with his hand, Stanley made a choking sound and slid into a chair. Sarah grasped his shoulders to comfort him. Then, motioning Hank and Emily to sit at the table, Sarah poured coffee for everyone.

Hank spoke with an unsteady voice. "I guess it's up to me to tell about it. I was the only one who was near enough. But I can tell you only a little." He glanced at Sarah, who nodded. He leaned forward, elbows on the table, his shoulders hunched. "It's about the net that Mr. Strauss had hung beneath the bridge to prevent workers from falling into the bay."

"Yes," whispered Sarah.

"There were two platforms, called strippers, that rolled the men along under the bridge. The platforms were attached to the floor beams, and workers rode them to pull away planking that had been used as forms for the concrete roadway.

"This morning, there were eleven men on the platform near the north tower of the bridge. Two more men, picking up debris, were in the net below.

"They moved the platform, and after it stopped, there was a loud crack. I wasn't too close to the platform, but I heard the crack. The bridge, where I stood, sort of shuddered. Some others and I started running, and all of a sudden, there was a sound like a clap of thunder. We ran as close as we dared and looked over the side of the bridge."

Hank stopped as if gaining strength to go on. Emily watched him, and Sarah saw empathy in her eyes. After a sip of coffee, he continued.

"It was horrible. That big platform, sixty feet long, dropped into the net. It was too much. The net was only meant to hold men, not a platform that weighed five tons. They said the whole thing, platform, men, and equipment, tipped to the side and fell into the net. Evidently the platform let go of the rail it traveled on.

"We ran to the other side of the bridge. Below, we could see several men hanging onto the net. The wind was so strong it waved the net like a piece of fabric. Everything went down, trapping the men in the net and hitting them. . . crushing some. They tried to get free of the net and debris, but they hadn't a chance."

Hank continued in a hoarse voice. "Only three men made it. One, who was rescued by a fishing boat, had a dead man in his arms. He didn't dare let go until he knew for sure the man was gone. When the platform fell, another man jumped aside and held onto a girder with his hands until they got a wire rope around him and pulled him up. He hung there for seven minutes! Can you imagine?" His face was pale. "The only other man pulled from the water had multiple external and internal injuries. I don't know if he'll make it."

Hank wiped his eyes. "I saw the faces of those men going down. . .and. . .and. . .they were so. . .scared," he said, covering his eyes as if to erase the horror.

Clay's sobs began again. Sarah and Emily prayed for all of them. The men needed God's strength just to get through the rest of the day. Sarah thought about Tim. Any minute he would come in from the school playground. What would they tell him?

"Ten men killed," said Sarah. "Think of all those families." She laid her hand on Stanley's. "Can we go to prayer meeting tonight? There may be church families affected."

"Yes, we must go. Not only for them but for ourselves. Clay, I want you to come with us. Times like these are when we especially need to assemble ourselves together. I didn't know any of the men. Did you?" Clay shook his head, and Stanley went on. "Then we have to help those who need help. The church will most likely know the families and the relatives affected."

"Okay, Dad," said Clay, wiping his eyes.

"What's the matter, Clay? Why are you crying?"

It was Tim.

Sarah felt sick. He looked so young standing in the doorway with his schoolbooks. How could they tell him? Hank came to the rescue again. He held out his arms, and Tim came to him.

"There was a bad accident on the bridge, Tim," he said, hugging him. "Some men were killed. We're all sad about it."

"Oh," Tim said in a tiny voice, "that's why my teacher was crying."

"Some of the men might be connected with our church

family," said Stanley. "We're going to prayer meeting, Tim."

Tim nodded. *He's handling it well,* Sarah thought, but she'd keep an eye on him.

Stanley spoke again. "Hank, more than anything, I'd like you to come with us. You're not a child or my son, like Tim, but I think it would help you live with this if you came along with us tonight."

"Please, Hank," said Emily.

Tim put his arm around Hank's neck. "Would you, Hank? I feel like Dad. I'd like it more than anything."

Hank looked around at the expectant faces and back to Tim. "I guess I will, Tim. It looks like I'll be hurting all of you if I don't." *Besides,* he thought, *I've got to be with them.*

&

One church member had a death in the extended family; some were connected distantly or by friendship. Though the congregation was in shock, Hank felt a sincere welcome from the people.

Shaking his hand, their pastor recognized Hank's name the minute he was introduced. Emily stood near, her blue eyes shining, but holding Hank's hand in a possessive grip was Tim. He was like a shadow that wouldn't go away.

Hank realized the Andersons were well-liked; no, they were well-loved. In fact, he saw enormous affection between all the people as they visited together before the service. Then a small choir assembled to sing a song he'd heard before. His warm reception had, for a few minutes, eased today's tragedy from his mind, but not for long. Had these people forgotten already?

Stepping to the pulpit, the pastor said in a quiet voice, "Today, we had a terrible tragedy on the bridge. One of our members lost a cousin. I knew him. The man had been a Christian. On an ordinary day, lost and troubled, he met Jesus

Christ, and he invited Him into his heart. After that, he lived his life in Christ as if every day would be his last. Today, it was."

The statement hit Hank with a jolt.

Friends of the fallen workers requested prayer for the families of the men, and the pastor read the names of all ten. After each name, a member offered prayer for that man's loved ones. The prayers were so heartfelt, Hank couldn't keep from being affected. Over and over in his mind played a single thought: *It could have been me.*

After the service, people lingered as if they could not bear to leave each other. With Tim still at his side, Hank sat in one of the pews, thinking. He remembered the pastor describing the dead man as "lost and troubled" before he came to Christ. He knew what that was like. At the present moment, he had never felt more lost. Around him members of the church were relating to each other on a level unknown to him. They were encouraging, sympathizing, grieving, rejoicing in turn, and he had no notion of how it was happening. He glanced down into Tim's eyes. He smiled and had a clever remark all ready, when Tim spoke instead.

"You know what the pastor meant by being lost, don't you, Hank? I'll bet that's the way you feel."

Hank chuckled. "What makes you think that, sprout?"

Tim's brow creased. "I'm serious, Hank. You feel lost, don't you?"

"Sometimes." He couldn't lie to the kid.

"That's because you need Jesus. I felt lost, too, before I gave my heart to Him."

"You see, Tim, that's the difference. I'm a grown-up man, and you're a little boy. You needed to do that."

"So do you, Hank. It doesn't make any difference to Jesus

how old you are." Tim stood. "I'm going away for a while, so you can think. Will you, Hank? Will you think about it?"

Hank was so surprised he could only stare straight ahead. His thoughts were fragmented. He felt as if someone had taken an eggbeater to his brain.

He'd seen grown men cry and curse and throw things that day because they couldn't deal with the accident. He'd taken a change of schedule to a *Chronicle* photographer shooting pictures with a reporter on assignment at the site. The same reporter ended up sending in news of the tragedy, and Hank couldn't have cared less that it wasn't his byline.

His only concern had been for Stanley and Clay, Emily's loved ones. And though it was unlikely they were involved, he wanted to see for himself. Then, when he knew they were safe, he had to be with Emily. He had seen Clay disoriented to the point of tears, blaming God for the deaths of the workmen. Yet, tonight, he had asked God's forgiveness before the whole church and made a statement that caused men and women to shed tears.

Clay would be another Stanley, doing good where it counted. Stanley, Sarah, and Emily were busy now, offering consolation and helping plan meals that would be taken to those in grief. Hank decided they were doing what they thought Jesus wanted done.

Only days ago, he had listened to Diane tell him how wrong he was to love Emily and her family. She had raised doubts in his mind. If not for Diane's manipulating, it would never have happened. *There's something evil about that girl,* Hank thought. *She's beyond help.*

That thought would shock Tim. Other people would say Hank Garrett was beyond help. Yet here was this kid, so concerned about him he'd put pride in his pocket and, red-faced, told his friend, Hank, straight out, that he needed to let Jesus come into his heart. What a kid.

Hank was so deep in thought he hadn't noticed the crowd dispersing. He looked around, feeling self-conscious, and saw Emily's family and the pastor praying together. They were praying for him! What was he going to do now? The lump in Hank's throat almost choked him. There was nothing else to do; he had a decision to make.

"Pastor?"

The gray, middle-aged man came to him. "Yes, Hank?"

Hank had a hard time starting. "I got put off religion when I was a kid. But Tim and the Andersons think I should *invite* Jesus Christ into my heart. Maybe it's the answer to the lost feeling I have. Will you help me?"

※

Clay knocked on the Grants' front door and stepped back. He heard footsteps, and Celia's father, short and muscular, appeared in the doorway of the bungalow-style house.

"Clay! Come in. Celia didn't tell me you were coming." He clasped Clay's shoulder. "Terrible thing that happened on the bridge today."

"Yes, sir." Clay said nothing more, and Mr. Grant did not press him.

They walked through the house to the covered patio outside the north door, where Mrs. Grant, Celia, and her two younger sisters sat talking in hushed voices. Pink and white periwinkles bloomed in planters at the patio's edge, and the faint fragrance of roses drifted from the lawn. Celia stood and came forward, her eyes probing Clay's.

"Are you all right."

"Yes, I am, now."

Mr. Grant motioned to his wife and the girls. "Why don't

we leave Celia and Clay alone and finish our devotion time inside?"

Tiny Mrs. Grant tiptoed to give Clay a warm hug as she went by him, then she followed the girls inside.

Celia caught Clay's hand. "Shall we sit here?" she asked, pointing to a white wicker settee. "Since you called, we've heard the names of the men who died. Did you know any of them?"

"No, neither Dad nor I knew them, but people in our church did. One family lost a cousin." He took her hand in both of his. "I had to come, Celia. I had to talk to you."

When he didn't go on, she scooted toward him. "What is it, Clay?"

"This has been a turnaround day in my life, Celia."

"I can imagine."

"When the accident happened, I was testing the engine of one of the boats they use to shuttle back and forth from the San Francisco side to the Marin side. It stalled on me, and I had a clear view of the whole thing. No one knows that but you."

"Oh, Clay." Celia snuggled against his side.

"I saw the platform pull loose—the noise had caused me to look up, and it fell into the net. The net pulled loose with a sound like machine gun shots. Men started dropping. Some slid off the platform and went down. Others hung onto the net. But there was no safety there. Everyone on the bridge was shouting and screaming. They were hysterical."

Clay swallowed a sob. "There was nothing anyone could do. I saw maybe one or two other boats, and they tried, but it was too late for most of the men. They drowned or died from their injuries. I wasn't close enough to see their faces like Hank did. I don't think I could have stood that. What I did see was bad enough."

Tears brimmed Celia's eyes. "If I could, I'd make it go away for you. But only God can do that. We'll pray He'll ease your pain, and I know He will."

Clay winced. "Celia, do you know what my first thought was?"

"No."

"Why did God let those men die? What's worse, I said it in front of my mother when I got home. I'm not trying to excuse myself, but I'd never witnessed men dying. I've never been to war or where there was a killing. I couldn't understand.

"I went by the office and told Dad I was going home. On the way, I held the tears back. I wouldn't let myself cry. No one knew my heart was breaking, but I was dying inside. I kept seeing the net fall, with men hanging on or dropping off."

"Clay, I understand. I do. Believe me. Who can say how anyone would react to such a thing?"

"I had the rest of the day and tonight to think about what I said. Mother and Dad made us all go to prayer meeting. Hank had brought Dad and Emily home, and he went with us. I wished for you, Celia. The Spirit of God moved in such a wonderful way tonight."

Clay sat forward with clasped hands. "I testified to what I had done and asked God's forgiveness. I rededicated my life to the Lord. On February 17, 1937, I rededicated my life to the Lord, and the one person I wanted to share it with was you."

He sat up straight and looked deep into Celia's eyes. "I want you with me all my life, Celia. I don't have anything to offer you now. But I love you, and I'm going to work hard to make something of myself for God and for you."

"What more could a girl ask for?" she asked, touching his cheek. "I love you too, Clay, and as long as we put God first, it will work out."

Clay pulled her close and kissed her forehead. "God's working it out for Emily and Hank, too. He was saved tonight. He realized he could die as suddenly as those men. It woke him up, and he asked the Lord into his heart. I would have told you sooner, but I had to share my own miracle first."

"So much good out of tragedy." She sighed. "How many other lives will this affect? How many will find the Lord because of a terrible accident? God is a great God, Clay. He takes a human mistake and works miracles."

twelve

"Did I wake you?" Hank said, with a smile in his voice.

"You know you did, you sadist! Mother called me. She's getting my breakfast ready now." Smiling, Emily changed the receiver of the handheld phone to her other ear and settled more comfortably into her dad's chair. "Why are you up and charming at this hour of the morning?" she said after a glance at the clock.

"Oh, charming, am I? Why, I'm always charming at. . . what time is it, anyway?"

"I'm not awake yet, but I think the big hand's on twelve and the little hand's on seven. You were with me until one o'clock last night. Where are you getting your energy?"

"Sweetheart, I woke up in a new world this morning, and I wanted yours to be the first voice I heard."

"Oh, Hank, how wonderful. God is so good to me!"

"To me, too. I'm going to buy a Bible. In fact, I'm going to buy two. One for my office and one for my apartment. I have a lot of catching up to do." She heard him moving around. "Look at that beautiful morning. The city is gorgeous out there!"

Pulling back the lace panel, she let in warm rays of sun. "You're right, the city is gorgeous. But I have an added bonus. Mother's frying bacon and eggs, and the aroma from the kitchen is incredible. Come and have some," she begged.

"There's no place I'd rather be, but I can't. I'm going out to the bridge site to get a consensus of emotion from some of the workers." He hesitated, and Emily waited. "I'm approaching them with a different attitude today, sweetheart. Before, my work was just stories—just a job. Today, I feel the hearts of those men, and I know Jesus is responsible. He's changed my life, Emily. I can't prove it yet, but I will. I feel like I've been reborn."

"Would you be surprised to know those same words have been said by thousands of people before you?"

"No, not if they felt the way I do. But no one has ever felt as good as I feel right now. It's impossible! I want to tell every person I come in contact with about Jesus. I know now what they're missing if they don't know Him!"

Emily sat back and smiled, delighted.

&

"Who were you talking to so early?" asked Sarah as she served Emily's plate of bacon and eggs. "No, don't tell me. It was that handsome, new Christian we know and love, wasn't it?"

Beaming, Emily nodded and sat to eat. "The very same. But now I have to get a move on, or I'll be late for school. Thank you, Mother." She took a biscuit Sarah offered from the pan kept warm on top of the oven. Buttering a flaky half, she finished it. "Seems strange to be happy after that terrible day yesterday. But, Hank was saved! I just can't be anything else."

"I understand, dear. We're all happy about Hank. And Timmy—God clearly has a plan of service for Tim's life. With Clay's rededication too, it was a night of an outpouring of God's blessings. My heart is singing today."

"I know." Emily took another biscuit and left two.

"Tim should be getting up anytime." Sarah pulled a loaf pan from the cabinet. "I'm getting food ready for the family of the Fosters' cousin. The pastor's coming by to get it at eleven o'clock. With the dishes of other ladies from church and my chicken and banana-nut bread, it should be a nice meal."

"Wish I could help, but my first graders won't let me off."

Emily finished her coffee, kissed her mother, and by eight o'clock she was out of the house.

❧

Hank came back to work that afternoon to find Diane waiting in front of the building.

"What are you doing here, Diane? Car trouble again?"

"I'm chasing you down. You're never home," she snapped.

"Diane, you can't be unaware of the tragedy at the bridge. I've been very busy. Why did you want to see me?"

"To work out what we're going to do. You were going to get back with me. Remember?"

"But I wasn't—"

"I know, you weren't convinced, but that's only because we haven't talked enough." Diane lowered her voice. "The other night we talked about how much we have in common and how right we are for each other. You let me believe you agreed with me."

"No, I said I'd think it over, and you should do the same."

Frowning, her voice turned strident. "You've had plenty of time to think it over. Now, *do* something." Diane stepped close, whispering, "You know I love you, Hank. We're alike. I told you—I'll never make you go to church. That's for Emily and her countrified ideas—not us. Oh, Hank, it would be so marvelous." Looking up with soulful eyes, she grabbed his hand and kissed it.

Hank felt embarrassed, yet he pitied Diane. Her life was based on nothing but her own desires. She believed an hour's conversation with him would make him fall in love with her.

He had to tell her his good news. In fact, he could hardly wait.

"I'm sorry if you thought everything was decided, Diane. I have something to share with you. Let's go where we can talk."

Down the street was a small cafe the news staff called "the greasy spoon," and when Hank took Diane inside she chose a booth in the back. He ordered coffee and watched her fidget in the seat opposite while he gathered his thoughts.

Dealing with the mental stress of the bridge men today was miles from trying to reason with a hysterical girl. Theirs was a real crisis, requiring every ounce of courage they could rally. One or two had even accepted his first invitations to church. Diane was a problem he hadn't anticipated.

Lord, he prayed in silence, *I'm not good at this yet, but I've come up against a real obstacle. Help me make Diane understand what's happened to me, and help her understand there can never be anything between us.*

Hank drank half his coffee while Diane added several spoonfuls of sugar and even more cream to hers.

"This will be a shock to you," he started. "I was with Emily's family after the accident yesterday, and I went to church with them last night."

Diane stopped stirring her coffee and burst out laughing. "Oh, Hank! You didn't!"

He remained calm. "This isn't a joke. I'm a Christian. I gave my heart to Jesus Christ."

The laughter left her face. "Are you crazy? You actually fell for that line? Come on, Hank."

"Yes, and I've never been happier. I'd like to tell you about it. Jesus can change your life as He did mine."

"Why should I want to change? I have a swell life!" She grabbed his hand. "Hank, you were just sentimental after what happened yesterday. Forget about it! Now that you're back to normal you'll realize you made a mistake. I know you will."

Trembling, she let his hand go. She started to say more but stopped. In a moment she slid out of the booth. "All right, Hank, have it your way. I'll wait. Do you hear? When you come to your senses, you call me, and we'll go on with our plans. Nothing's changed. Not for me. Remember that!"

A tear stole down her cheek; she swiped it away in a frenzy. Looking straight ahead, she hurried to the door. Hank watched sadly as she disappeared from his view. Diane was so lost. Just as lost as he had been.

&

A week later, Hank took Emily to their favorite ice cream parlor. He had acquired a closed sedan after the bridge accident, so Emily no longer had to grab a scarf when they went out.

Enlarged color prints of San Francisco's landmarks decorated the walls of the shop, which was painted a cool, light green and white. As usual, Hank and Emily took their favorite table near the plate-glass window on the side and ordered strawberry sodas. His hand reached across the table to capture hers.

"Are we going to the pie supper after the Sunday night service?" he asked, arresting her blue gaze.

"Yes. I was hoping you wouldn't have to work."

"How will your pie be wrapped, so I'll know which one to bid on?"

"Now, Hank, you know I can't tell. That wouldn't be fair."

His palm stroked her cheek. "It wouldn't be fair to make me eat some other girl's lemon pie. It couldn't possibly be as good as yours."

She smiled and leaned her face against his hand. "How do you know I'll make a lemon pie? It could be chocolate."

"Naah. I saw a row of lemons on the windowsill above the kitchen sink. Your mom put them there to ripen for you, didn't she?" He grinned at her. "She knows what I like."

Emily couldn't deny that; both her parents loved Hank. "Yes, Mother likes to see you happy."

Hank chuckled. "I guess we'll eat together at Will's next Saturday night, too," he said, smiling at a little girl, licking to keep ahead of the drips on her ice cream cone.

"I don't understand, Hank. They refuse our invitations, and we haven't been invited to their house since we left. I don't think they're too happy with us right now, for some reason." Emily wondered why Hank frowned. "What is it, Hank?"

"I got a phone call from your Uncle Will. He wants me to come for supper that night. I supposed you'd be there, too."

Although she didn't like the sound of it, Emily had no right to intrude. Hank's life was his own. Will's reason for seeing him might have nothing to do with Diane. Diane? Why had her cousin popped into her mind? Hank had already explained their only problem involving her.

"It could be a story opportunity in relation to his business," she said. "I expect he hears a lot of yarns that would make good stories."

"Maybe. You've got my curiosity up now. It'll be interesting to see what he's got on his mind."

❧

Hank didn't dress up for his invitation to dinner; Will had said nothing to indicate that he should. With smiling dignity, Lee swung back one of the carved double doors to admit him and slipped a doorstop underneath to hold it. Later, Will and Hank took seats in the dining room to eat, surprising Hank.

"Did your ladies desert you tonight, sir?" Spreading his napkin over his lap, he checked Will's expression.

A wry smile swept Will's face. "Only temporarily. I expect they'll be here before you leave."

For a few minutes, they ate the breaded steak, potatoes, and the salad which Lee had served. Then, Will put down his fork, took a drink of iced tea, and cleared his throat.

"I've asked you here for a particular reason, Hank. I want to clear the air on a certain matter." The announcement alerted Hank's thinking, and tension mounted as Will continued. "Diane is quite fond of you. But I'm sure you know that."

"She says she is, sir, but I—"

"Tell you what, Son, let's not make any impulsive statements we might regret."

Hank frowned. "I don't understand, sir. What impulsive statement are you afraid I'll make?" Hank was beginning to suspect the purpose of his invitation.

"Diane and I had a long talk last night. It happened because I found her lying on her bed, crying—weeping as if her little heart would break. In fact, she seemed at the point of illness. I tell you, it almost broke this old father's heart of mine," he said with a heavy sigh.

Hank thought Will's statement a little dramatic. "I'm sorry to hear that."

"I was, too. Sorry to hear that the reason for her tears was you." Will sipped from his glass, staring at Hank. "She tells me you had dinner together not long ago, at which time you more or less agreed that the two of you had much in common."

"Mr. Anderson—"

"*And*," cut in Will, "to the best of her knowledge, it was understood that you would think over the facts with the idea that you and she become engaged in the near future."

Hank's first impulse was to yell his denial, but he kept his temper and answered calmly. "No, sir. That's a misconception on her part. Diane has the unfortunate habit of thinking what she wants is what everyone else wants. In this case, it's not true."

Will was indignant. "My daughter is a very beautiful girl, Hank. She wouldn't have to beg a man to marry her. If she says you two had an understanding, I believe there was one."

Much as he disliked himself for it, Hank was angry. "You have my word, sir, we do not have an understanding, and I can tell you why. I'm in love with your niece, Emily. I have been for months. Diane knew it and gave Emily's religion as one of the reasons she and I were better suited. It didn't work."

"Well, that's a shock. I can't imagine any man choosing Emily over Diane. What does Emily have that Diane doesn't?"

The time had come, and Hank was glad it was here. "I can give you her most important asset. Emily is a Christian."

Food forgotten, Will threw back his head and laughed. "That's an asset? From Hank Garrett, the town's number one critic of religion? You've even hinted at its flaws in print. Diane said you agreed the two of you had that in common."

Smiling, Hank felt the Lord with him. "Evidently Diane failed to tell you—I've accepted Jesus Christ as my Savior, Mr. Anderson. The night of the bridge accident, I realized I was a lost man and needed the Lord. Everyone does. Even you."

"Don't include me! I don't need that. But just hold on a minute, we're not through. Maybe we can balance this out."

Will rose and paced the room. Thinking they had finished their meal, Lee came in to clear away dishes. Will gave him an indignant wave off and moved to Hank's side. Looking down at him, Will's tone turned commanding.

"If you are what my daughter wants, I'll give you twenty-five thousand dollars to marry her."

The telephone in the living room rang.

Hank stood. Lowering his head, he shook it slowly in disbelief. He looked up and faced his host directly.

"Mr. Anderson, I love Emily, not Diane. No amount of money in the world can change that." He took his keys from his pocket. "I'm going. I'd rather not be here when Diane returns."

Leaving the dining room, he saw Lee put the receiver down on the telephone table.

"Telephone for you, sir," he said to Will.

For a few seconds Will didn't move. Glaring at Hank, he crossed the room to pick up the phone, and Hank left by the open front door.

"Yes?" Will said into the phone.

Continuing across the veranda, Hank had reached the steps when he heard a name through the open front door that stopped him. He backtracked silently to listen.

"Maroni? What is it?" Will paused. "Well, yes, if I have to." Another pause. "Can't you handle it yourself?" A longer pause. "No! Don't do that—you'll be seen. Just stick tight where you are, and I'll meet you at the club at one o'clock."

Hank slipped out to his car. A suspicious period of time had elapsed, so he shoved the gearshift into neutral and pushed until the car began to move. He jumped in and guided it down the drive. At the street, he started the motor and drove down the block to a spot hidden by shadows. He could still see the house. When Will Anderson came out, he intended to follow him.

This night could put together all his legwork since last year. He'd come up with one dead end after the other trying to figure Maroni's operations, Clay's little adventure, and that club out in the sticks. He'd almost let go of it once Clay was clear, but now he was glad he hadn't. He had a friend at the SFPD. If this trip didn't turn out to be a dry run, he would lay out the facts he had gathered for the officer's scrutiny.

At six minutes past midnight, Will's car came down the drive and headed in the direction opposite to the way Hank was parked. Hank turned around and followed at a safe distance. There was traffic, but not enough to keep him from trailing Will.

He had a pretty good idea what route Will would take, but he had to be absolutely sure, and the best way was to follow right behind. He checked the gas gauge and was sure he'd be okay.

It was foggy now. Hank had to get closer to keep from losing his man. He was turning. That wasn't according to plan. Then he got it. They were approaching Will's produce building. When they reached it, he parked and watched Will unlock a garage and change to the car with the broken taillight. *Nice touch,* Hank thought. *A different car for each of his lives.*

They reached the nightclub fifteen minutes early. Hank stopped at the side of the blacktop road and waited until he was sure Will had time to park. Edging ahead, he watched for Will, but he didn't see him go in. There must be a private entrance.

Hank circled the building slowly. Jazz dance music blared into the night. He spotted Will's car, almost invisible under a vine-covered slot. Driving to the edge of the parking lot, he found an excellent position to keep an eye on the hidden car.

Emily! If it turned out that Will was linked to misconduct, she and her family would be affected. She was loyal; she might never speak to Hank again. His heart almost stopped. Should he go on? Yes. He had no choice; he had to bring in his story. He was a Christian now, determined to be an honest reporter.

He scrunched down behind the steering wheel as a couple came around the corner of the building and made their way to an expensive looking car. Both had been drinking. They laughed hilariously at the ineptitude of the man as he un-locked the vehicle.

A black limousine rolled into sight and stopped near Will's car. Hank saw the chauffeur get out and open the back door.

The man at the sports car called out, "There 'e iss now!" He and the woman laughed. "Sorry, old pal," he yelled. "You had bad luck thish time. We won two thousand off those babies this afternoon. Ran for me 'stead of you! Haw, haw! Came to letcha get a li'l back, but we're goin' now. S' long!"

The chauffeur, who had tried to silence the man, now threatened him with harsh words. At the same time a big man in a dark suit, his hat pulled low over his forehead, slipped from the back seat of the limousine. He disappeared through a secluded opening near Will's car.

Hank recognized Maroni at once. It was all coming together. With what he had just heard he could take the story to his friend at the police department and let the real work begin.

thirteen

By the second week in April, Hank faced an enormous problem. It was time to tell Emily's family that he was responsible for the charges brought against Will for running an illegal racetrack bookmaking operation.

Hank's dogged persistence culminated in a raid by police on the nightclub where Will Anderson was exposed as the silent partner of Frederico Maroni, illegal alien. In the basement of the club was a bank of telephones and an office staff carrying on a million-dollar business. Not only the rich, but the homeless and hungry gambled in an attempt to win a fortune. A shameless business; Hank's gratitude that it no longer existed overshadowed what he had to do.

After work, Hank drove to Stanley's house. He could imagine the Andersons' reaction. They must be reverberating from the reports on the radio and in the *Chronicle*. Hank's byline had not been used; the paper said only that the gambling operation was uncovered by one of their staff. Few would connect Emily's modestly living family with the flamboyant Will Anderson family in Ingleside Terrace. Yet her family would still suffer.

Hank felt like a man who had cut his own throat. The story broke just as he was ready to ask Emily to marry him. Would the unsavory business tear them apart? That couldn't happen. Since he'd accepted Christ, he had dreamed daily of serving the Lord with Emily as his wife.

She'd invited him to eat supper with them, that night, but Hank had declined. How could he drop such a confession on them after eating a delicious meal Emily and Sarah had prepared?

As he left the car and walked to the house, Emily came running to meet him. They caught hands.

"Oh, Hank, I'm so glad to see you. I know you've been busy, or you would have called. I hesitated to call you for the same reason. It's been terrible. Dad hardly says a word, and Mother is so worried about him she doesn't talk either." Emily clutched his arm. "Come into the house. Dad has a soft spot for you. Mother, too. They'll be glad you're here."

"I'm not sure they—"

"Hank!" Clay flew down the walk to join them. "Boy, are we in a mess. I guess Emily's given you the picture— it's a good thing you came."

"Let's go in, Clay. I don't want the folks to look out and see us talking without them." Emily led the way to the house.

Inside, Sarah and Stanley sat together in their chairs. They looked up and spoke to Hank as the three appeared. Tim was nowhere to be seen. No one said a word; the silence multiplied Hank's tension. Finally, Stanley raised his head.

"This has been a trying week for me, Hank," he said. "God has sustained me with work that had to be done. Otherwise, I think I'd have gone crazy. My own brother! I still can't believe it. It has to be a mistake!

"We had the same beginnings. . .sons of a moderate-means Christian family. But Will always yearned to be *somebody*. That's how he put it. That's why he came to California in the first place. He wanted to get ahead, and the opportunities were here. Now, he has nothing. I'm glad our parents are with the Lord, so they don't have to bear the shame."

Sarah clasped his hand in hers. "It will be all right. Remember, Paul said to the Corinthians, 'Watch ye, stand fast in the faith. . .' We *will* stand fast in the faith, Stanley. God will see us through." She pulled her gaze from his. "Have a seat, Hank. Would you like something to drink? Coffee or iced tea? Emily will get it for you."

"No, thanks," he said, "I came to talk. . .to all of you." Hank took a chair beside Stanley. "Please believe me. I prayed a long time for courage to face you. You may hate me after this, but here it is. Stanley, I'm the one who blew the whistle on Will."

Stanley gasped. "Hank! You? How—?"

"Hear me out, please. Then, if you want me to leave, I will."

"Yes, tell us," said Sarah, taking her hand from her mouth. "We need to hear it straight from you."

"I was after Maroni. I had no idea Will would figure into it. I'd heard complaints on the Embarcadero about a worker's alliance that was pulling young unemployed men like Clay into the Communist movement. I thought Maroni was mixed up in it."

"That's true, Mother, Dad. He told me," said Emily.

"My friend, Charlie, came along at just the right time, and he took Clay away from a bad scene and gave him a job."

"I'm really grateful, Hank. I want you to know that."

Hank knew then that Clay had told his father the whole story.

He nodded. "That union stuff brought Maroni to my attention, but then, things changed. He maneuvered Clay into driving him to the nightclub, and I'd had hints of a secret partner. I had to learn who *he* was. Without realizing it, Clay helped by mentioning that Will at least knew about the club." He watched Emily weakly lower herself into a chair.

Clay had dropped to the floor and leaned back against

doorpost. Biting his lip, he seemed deep in thought. When Hank paused, he spoke up. "I remember asking Diane once where her dad got all his money. She had a hissy fit and told me she wished people would stop asking her that. Evidently I wasn't the only one."

"It ate at me, too," said Hank. "How could he afford all he had with only a market shed downtown? I started checking on his investments but could find nothing. Apparently people got paid to cover them up. Money is a grand persuader."

"But how did you discover he was Maroni's partner, and that they ran such a rotten business?" Emily asked, frowning.

This was the part Hank dreaded. "Will had me over to dinner. Only he and I were there, and he had a deal he thought would interest me." He looked straight at Emily. "It didn't."

From the little smile she returned, Hank knew she realized that the "deal" was Diane. But she trusted him—no questions asked. He felt he couldn't love her more.

"As I was leaving, Will got a phone call. He said Maroni's name, and outside, I slipped back to the door to listen. You may think that was dishonest, but something compelled me to do it. Will said he'd meet Maroni at the club at one o'clock.

"I followed him, and he went to the club. Then Maroni arrived. God let me hear a customer address Maroni with remarks that gave me a whole new angle on his activities. The nightclub was a gambling house with an off-track betting operation. With what I already had, I took it to the police for investigation.

"That's it. The police did the rest. In my defense, I have to say this: Those two were making money off rich, unsaved people, but they were also making it off poor souls who had caught the fever and were robbing their families of necessities in order to gamble. It was a dirty business, Stanley."

The older man rubbed tears from his eyes. "You were right, Hank. It was the right thing to do. If the Lord isn't honored with honesty and hard work, we can't blame Him when He punishes those who disobey and rebel against Him."

Hank breathed easier with Stanley's forgiveness, and to his relief, they talked no more of Will's situation. Hank stayed until his eyes were heavy. His last week's activity had cost hours of lost sleep. Emily rose to go out with him. Clay, too. Clay talked as they walked along. "Hank, Uncle Will broke the law deliberately. You acted according to the law. Dad knows."

"Thanks, Clay. That makes me feel better." They shook hands. "Say—what's happening with you and that red-haired charmer? Did you throw her over for a new one?"

"Never. Celia's it!"

Hank sensed that this was the first Emily had heard of Clay's intentions. She closed her eyes as if in thanks.

"Tell us, Clay," she murmured then, hugging his waist. "Have you asked Celia to marry you?"

"What do I have to offer, Em? I have no money. She could keep her job for a while, but what if we had a baby? I can't support her, let alone three of us. My job seems secure, yet it will be years before I save enough money to marry."

His plight touched Hank's heart and pushed him further toward a decision he felt God was leading him to make.

Clay gave Hank a playful punch on the shoulder. "Thanks again. I guess I'll go in and let you and Emily talk. I know how hard this was for you. You're a true friend."

Emily looked after him. "Isn't he a good guy? He's always helping people. Remember the school chaperone with car trouble? Clay wasn't satisfied until he had her car working like new."

"Yeah. Too bad he's so discouraged about his prospects."

"Seems like we'll be poor forever. We all work as hard as we can and still barely make it." Emily shook her head. "Would you listen to me? God has given us blessing upon blessing, and I'm griping." She smiled. "Who knows? Maybe He has something right around the corner for Celia and Clay."

❧

Emily's despair was not lost on Hank. He thought about Emily and her family almost constantly. The paper sent him to Los Angeles to interview a pediatrician whose research with infantile paralysis in children was gaining attention. He stopped overnight with his parents and learned Frances was engaged.

"We're not too happy with the match." His father set the last bulb in a pot and added more soil. Hot sun beamed through the glass of the greenhouse. His father's forehead gleamed with perspiration. "We think he's after her money."

Hank wiped his own forehead. "I know this guy. He may be."

Mr. Garrett finished his planting, watered the pots, and put the tools away. He straightened to his full six-foot height and replaced his cap on his silver hair, dark eyes questioning.

"Tell me what you know."

Hank hardly hesitated. "His reputation's not the best. He's divorced and took away a lot of money from the deal, which he spent. I guess he's ready again." He opened the greenhouse door, and outside a cool breeze ventilated their damp clothes.

"Talk to your sister, Son. Maybe she'll listen to you," his father said, and Hank realized he was indeed worried.

Hank felt sorry for his father and mother. This time, they seemed old and vulnerable. Why hadn't he noticed before? Had Christ made the difference in his view of them? His ability to see their side of a story now instead of opposing every opinion had produced happier results on this visit. The Bible said to honor his parents, and obeying the Word had rescued their relationship. He spent an extra day in L.A. to be with his family.

&

After swimming in the back lawn kidney-shaped pool with his sister, he pulled himself out and held out his hand to assist her. "I've got something to say, Sis."

Frances pulled down the legs of her black, one-piece bathing suit. "Here it comes. The folks asked you to talk to me."

Hank sat on a stone bench and she joined him. "You're right, but the advice is my own. You're older than me, but I've been around the block a few times. This guy is bad news, Fran."

"I expected you to object, and if you'd come at me with a bunch of don'ts, I'd have told you to lay off. As it happens, I've about decided to call it off myself. I'm not ready."

Hank put his arm around her shoulders and squeezed, amused that she had chosen *almost* the same words he'd used earlier.

&

Before he left, Hank had his new car serviced, and his father went with him to the dealership where he'd bought it. Hank had opened two bottles of grape soda pop for them while they sat on folding chairs in the service area.

"I notice a big change in you, Son. What's going on?"

"What you've always wanted. I accepted Christ as my Savior after the Golden Gate Bridge accident. Right in front of me, death, ten times over, suddenly stared me in the eye."

"That would do it, all right. Your mother and I are changing too—old age seems to be mellowing us."

"No, I think God's doing it, for both of us. Nowadays I study my Bible, and its truth influences everything I do. Emily says I'm different, and she encourages me every day."

"You seem to care a great deal for her. Has she any money?" Hank glared at him. "Now, don't take offense. I wouldn't care if she's as poor as a church mouse. I merely wondered."

"Poor. I think that's a fair appraisal of her finances."

"What are your intentions toward her?"

"I'd like to marry her if she'll have me."

"Don't you think she will?" came his father's shocked reply.

Hank set his bottle down and leaned forward, hands clasped, his forearms on his knees. "I suppose this is as good a time as any, Father. I've been rethinking my refusal of Grandfather's trust money. At first, I wanted to show you and Mother I could make my living as a newsman. You were both so opposed to it, it went against the grain. Now I think I've proved it to all of us."

"Well, I'm ready to say we were wrong. One can hardly argue with awards and prizes for excellence in journalism."

"Thank you, Father." Hank's gratitude warmed his face. He took a sip of his drink. "I'm going to start using the money."

"Why not? Your grandfather would approve. Did Emily have anything to do with your accepting it?" Mr. Garrett asked warily.

Hank didn't mind this time. "She doesn't know about it. In fact, she doesn't know I belong to this family. Believe it or not, I won her simply as Hank Garrett, reporter. But I want to give her more than she has, and there's a special person some of the money could give a big lift to. Emily and her family are the kindest, most uncomplaining, most deserving people I've ever met. They live their lives in Christ—even Tim, her little brother. It was that young boy who influenced me to accept Christ that night."

"They've all had a vast influence. I'd like to meet them."

"Would you? I'd be more than happy to arrange it."

"Is that what you had in mind when you came?"

"No," said Hank, "I hadn't thought it out that far. I'd only thought about the money buying things for Emily that I can't afford. But I would like to get the two families together. I'd like that very much, Father."

"That's what we must do, then." His father was actually chuckling. "Frances goes East to a college reunion in May, and your mother and I will be by ourselves. Let's make it that weekend."

Thank You, Lord, Hank prayed. *You've made everything come out right.* Why had he waited so long to trust Him?

☙

The meeting took place at Stanley and Sarah's, followed by a Sunday afternoon feast. Mr. and Mrs. Garrett were driven from Los Angeles in their chauffeured automobile, and two maids ensconced them in a suite at the Mark Hopkins Hotel. Suffering his first attack of nerves ever, Hank drove them in his car, to an amiable Anderson welcome. The Mark Hopkins was never mentioned.

Emily had been jubilant at news of their coming. She and Sarah cleaned and polished to bring their home up to its highest level of charm. Finishing the last of the woodwork in the living room, Sarah pitched her scrubbing cloth into a bucket of cleaner.

"Oh, Emily, how I wish we had a fine dining room set. How will we ever serve dinner without embarrassing ourselves?"

"I've been thinking about this, Mother, and I have a plan. We'll bring the kitchen table into the dining room and cover it with the best linen tablecloth, hemmed to floor-length size.

It will be perfect. You and Dad will have a special dining area with Hank's parents."

Sarah was almost dancing for joy at Emily's solution.

"Celia and I have already talked, and she's bringing a tub of flowers from their garden. When we add candles and fresh flowers, it will give the room a. . .a *delicate splendor,*" Emily mimicked, her hands encircling an imagined space. She and Sarah giggled. "By placing more candles and flowers around the house, we'll transform our little home into a shining jewel! And that's not a joke," Emily said proudly.

Outside of being surprised at their elegance, Emily responded to the Garretts as she did to any guest. As herself. Instantly at ease with Emily and her family, Hank's parents seemed to throw away their reserve.

Celia joined them for lunch, and the young people ate at the outside picnic table. Tim sat on a nail keg at the end.

"Do we have everything we need?" Emily surveyed the table.

Hank reached for her hand. "Will you sit down and eat? You haven't stopped since we got here."

"Yeah, Em. You're a regular whirling dervish!" Clay joked.

"I'll do the next course," said Celia. "Let's eat while we can. Say the blessing, Clay. Tim's about to starve."

Emily and Celia waited both tables, and the Garretts showed every evidence of enjoying their visit.

After lunch, Celia and Clay washed dishes, and Emily and Hank took charge in the living room. It was a profitable time. Conversation flowed. The two families had many things in common. Humor, anecdotes, religion, parenthood, the bridge: all were discussed in open-minded harmony.

The Garretts' hearts were totally captured by Tim. "You remind me so much of Hank when he was a boy. I expect you keep your mother busy trying to stay ahead of the mending, don't you?" asked Mr. Garrett.

"I don't know. Do I, Mom?" Tim lowered his voice and turned a serious face to the man. "She never complains. Not ever."

Mrs. Garrett laughed. "You're a fine boy, Tim. When Hank was your age, he and Frances were peas in a pod when it came to getting into trouble, but Hank was the one who apologized." She smiled. "He always had a tender heart."

"Emily has a tender heart, too!" said Tim, and Emily's face warmed, though she'd learned more about Hank to love.

Mrs. Garrett's arthritis forced them to leave, so she could take more medicine. Since they were going back to Los Angeles the next morning, Mrs. Garrett drew Emily to her side and extracted a promise from her.

"You must come to Los Angeles for a visit, Emily. I won't be satisfied until you and Frances meet. She's at a reunion this weekend, but we'll make sure she's at home when you come."

"I'd like that very much. I'm eager to meet her, too."

As Mrs. Garrett said good-bye to Sarah and Celia, Mr. Garrett took Emily's arm and walked her ahead of the others toward Hank's car.

His remark was a whispered one. "I'd like to give you a piece of advice, if you don't mind." He leaned close. "Don't let him get away, little girl. He needs you."

❧

A week later, Clay picked up a letter from the telephone table where his mother always left mail for the family. One heavy, official-looking envelope was addressed to him. Minutes later, he called Celia. He gasped for breath.

"Honey, are you sitting down? If you aren't, you'd better!"

"Clay! You got a raise!"

"Better than that!"

"Oh, I can't wait. Tell me. Please!"

"You won't believe it, Celia. In my hand I have a certified check for five thousand dollars that came in the mail! And the note with it says, *'This is to buy a garage of your own.'* It's signed, *'A Friend.'* " He took a deep breath. "Will you marry me, Ce—"

"Yes!"

fourteen

"Hurry up, Emily," called Tim. "Hank will be here any minute!"

Emily knew that, but everything was going wrong this morning. First, she'd had to mend a run in her stocking. Then, retrieving her walking shoes from under the bed, she stepped on her skirt hem and had to fix that. Last, a drawer stuck, and she'd broken a fingernail. She wanted to be waiting calmly in the living room when Hank came, but now she'd barely be ready.

Her dress was new. For this special day she'd bought a green-dotted swiss with a straight skirt and a wide self belt. White eyelet trimmed the dress, and it fit perfectly. The day would be warm, though, and she reached in the closet for a hat with a wider-than-average brim, for protection from the sun.

"Emily, do these shoes look all right with this dress?" Sarah said, standing in the doorway looking at her feet. "You remember, Hank said, 'Be sure to wear comfortable shoes.'"

"They look good, Mother." Emily turned in front of the mirror with a little smile. If Hank said it, it was mandatory. She turned back to her mother. "Now you tell me—am I put together? Everything's gone haywire this morning. I don't know what's the matter with me."

Sarah put on her teasing smile. "It couldn't be someone by the name of Hank Garrett, could it?"

"I am nervous for some reason," she said, smiling. "You may be right, but I think it's the day. *Pedestrian Day on the Golden Gate Bridge!* Just think, Mother. We get to walk across before cars are even allowed. Isn't that exciting? People all over the world would like to be in our shoes."

Tim ran in, out of breath but loud. "Hank came, and he said to tell you he was taking Clay to get Celia, and they'll be right back!"

"Lower your voice, Tim," said Sarah. "I think we got it."

"Can I go with you and Hank, Emily?"

"*May* I go with. . .so that's why I'm getting all these bulletins on Hank's whereabouts," she said, ruffling his hair.

"I think you'd better go with your dad and me." Tim clumped out, and Sarah asked, "Are Clay and Celia going with you?" She stepped behind Emily sitting at her dressing table.

"It's up to the rest of you to arrange how we get there. We'll all be together, anyway." Emily put on Tangee lipstick.

"I doubt either you *or* Clay will want the rest of us tagging along to slow you down."

"Hank and I don't mind. I can't speak for Clay and Celia. They're off on a distant star somewhere." She giggled. "How did your visit with Mrs. Grant turn out? Are the wedding plans complete yet?" Emily tweezed an errant eyebrow.

"Almost. Celia's a smart, sensible girl. She's planning her wedding with economy and good taste." Sarah moved to a window and looked out at the bright day. "God is so good to give her to us. She helped make her own dress, and yours is almost ready to be fitted. I love sewing with her mother. Clara and I seem to read each other's minds."

"Are they still having the wedding on the lawn?"

"Yes, and it will be beautiful. They have flowers of every color of the rainbow. The place simply begs to hold a wedding." Her mother straightened a gather on the embroidered muslin curtain, gave it a pat, and moved to sit on Emily's bed.

"It's wonderful the way things have worked out for them. I don't think I've ever seen a happier couple. I wish *A Friend* would do the same for Hank," said Emily without guile.

"Seems strange, Clay's getting married before you. I thought you'd be the one. I don't understand it. Hank acts like he can't stand to have you out of his sight, yet he doesn't seem in any hurry to marry. What do you think he's waiting for?"

"I'm not sure," Emily replied. "I only know if God wants us together, we will be. I just have to be patient. But until Hank's as sure as I am, I don't want a proposal."

Stanley, frowning, appeared at the door, "I'm distressed about Letitia and Diane. I called Letitia a few minutes ago and was told not to call back again."

"Oh, Stanley, I'm sorry it happened on such a happy day," said Sarah.

"They harbor a great deal of resentment toward our family. They think we should drop Hank from our acquaintance because his paper caught Will." Stanley sat on the bed beside Sarah.

"Sooner or later they'll come around, Stanley," she said, hugging him. "Don't blame yourself if they won't let you help them. They can't keep their house, but invested wisely, money from a big place like that should support them very well."

"Yes, it should. I've tried to get that over to them. If they'd let me, I know I could help. After all, I spent years in banking." He leaned forward, his forearms on his knees, his hand reaching for Sarah's. "I want to talk to them about the Lord too, but right now they wouldn't listen. They're convinced that the scandal was a mistake, that it will be cleared up, and that things will return to normal."

Emily got up and bent to kiss his cheek. "It's been so embarrassing for them, Dad. They're still in shock."

"Letitia has been seeing Will at the county jail, but Diane won't go. That girl has a lot of growing up to do. I pity her. Well, we won't give up, will we?"

Both women smiled at him.

"Say," he said, finding his own smile, "I'm going out with two of the prettiest girls in San Francisco today."

❧

Emily's day righted itself when Hank's eyes complimented her new dress. His blue seersucker suit was one Emily had not seen before, and he was so handsome she caught her breath. They had the whole day together! He would pick up items for a story, but that would add to, not detract from, the enjoyment of long hours together.

Tim decided on his own to go in Stanley's car, and no one but his sister knew the reason.

"Hank and Clay will be mooning over you girls all day," the boy said. "It's enough to make a guy puke!"

❧

All over San Francisco the celebration was in progress. The city, aware of crowning herself with greatness throughout the world, was decorated for the honor. Pedestrian Day was the beginning of a weeklong festival.

Hank guided his car through careless traffic and jay-walking citizens toward a parking area he hoped would not be filled.

"With the parade at Crissy Field," he said, motioning toward the Presidio, "there's activity all over town."

"But we can see a parade anytime. There's only one Pedestrian Day on the bridge, and I want to be part of it, don't you?" Emily's enthusiasm was contagious, making Hank smile, too.

She half turned in her seat and saw Clay kissing Celia. Hank glanced in the rearview mirror and chuckled at Emily's red face.

"I hope that doesn't shock you. They are practically married, you know," he said in an undertone.

"No, I'm not shocked. I just can't get used to my kid brother grown up." She giggled, then kept her voice low. "He's proving it every day. He's up and gone by six in the morning and doesn't come home until after dark. With the good name of the garage he bought, he inherited a few regular customers, and he intends to keep them."

"Will Celia work after they're married?"

"No, she wants to give it up to keep books for Clay."

"Is that what he wants?"

"I—"

"If you're going to talk about us, you may as well raise your voices so we can hear," Clay joked.

"We didn't want to, uh. . .*interrupt,*" said Hank.

Celia giggled. "It's all right," she said. "We can always reschedule. Oh! Hank, look! There's a car leaving! Park, quick! We can walk from here."

Hank grabbed the spot and the girls hopped out of the car.

"Would you check my stocking seams, Celia?" Emily asked. "Are they straight?"

Nodding an affirmative, Celia assessed Emily's total look. "I love your dress," she said. "Your blue maid of honor dress is a good color on you, too. In fact, I don't know of any color you can't wear. When you have red hair, you envy that."

"You shouldn't. That gold dress looks wonderful on you."

Clay faced them, hands on his hips. "Could we break up this mutual admiration society and get on to the bridge?"

The girls laughed, took the men's arms, and started out matching the their pace. Their progress slowed by the time they reached the bridge. Standing to the side of the six-lane roadway, all four took in the breathtaking scene.

Hundreds of wide-eyed people swarmed toward the two great towers of the bridge, painted a warm red. Joining the crowd, the couples stepped through a gate to walk on the bridge for the first time. Giant cables, hung over the towers, suspended the bridge magnificently over the deep blue-green water of San Francisco Bay. With a backdrop of Marin County hills, Emily thought it the most beautiful sight in the world.

"There are Mother and Dad!" she exclaimed. "How did we all manage to get here at the same time?"

"With thousands of people massed around us, I'd say it's a miracle," said Hank, pulling her toward her parents.

"We've been waiting for you," shouted Tim, bounding up to them. "Isn't this the berries?"

Until they decided what to do first, the group clustered at the side, letting the crowd rush by.

"I talked to one of the guards. Barriers on both sides of the bridge were lifted at six o'clock this morning," declared Stanley. "They admitted hundreds who waited hours to be the first."

Tim circled Emily twice. "Guess what we saw? A man playing a tuba! Up on the middle of the bridge, playing his tuba to beat the band!"

"Who'd you fool with that gag, squirt?" asked Clay, missing the confirming nods of his parents.

"Hold on, Clay. He's telling the truth," said Hank. "Some weird things will take place today. Remember, this is a chance to do *first* things on the Golden Gate Bridge. Six sprinters from the *Chronicle* are supposed to cross both ways, barefoot."

"Really?" said Emily, whose giggle stopped as she focused on a man riding a unicycle, playing a harmonica.

Laughing, the family started its own trip.

"How high are the towers, Hank?" said Emily, still smiling. "Give us some of that valuable research you've been collecting."

"They're over seven hundred feet. They taper upward to the height of a sixty-five-story building."

"Oooh! I get dizzy when I look straight up at something that high," said Celia. "Clay, look! Boy Scouts! Maybe their troop will be the first one to cross."

"I'll bet you're right. That's probably why they're spruced up in their uniforms. Someone should take their picture." Clay called to the rest, "Keep your eyes open, folks. Don't let us miss anything we haven't seen."

"You already did!" Tim marched ahead as if holding a tuba and sounded his oom-pah-pah until everyone tired of it.

"Come back, Tim," called Sarah. "You can practice at home."

Tim obeyed but he ran to the side, looked over and, at once, tried to climb up the side rail.

Emily darted after him with Hank right behind. "Tim, you'll

give Mother and me heart attacks if you don't stay close. Be a good boy, please."

"I have to second that, Tim," said Hank. "We want to make this a day to remember. It wouldn't do for you to have an accident."

"Okay, Hank." Tim looked contrite—at least for a moment. Hey! Lookie there!"

They turned to see a man on stilts walking ahead of a dog dressed in a tuxedo and a cat dressed as a ballerina, both on leashes. They tried not to laugh; it was serious business to the people attempting a *first*. But it was hopeless. A man walking backward contorting his face to the ridiculous was their downfall. Rejoining their group, they all burst out laughing.

"Help us get serious, Hank," said Stanley, chortling. "Tell us more about the bridge."

"Well, it's high enough so that the largest ship afloat can pass under it at high tide, and it's over three and a half miles long. Think we can walk it?"

All but Sarah claimed they could. "Look for me in the middle, eating a hot dog. We heard someone say they'll be selling them," she said, winking at Tim.

Celia giggled. "I may keep you company if it's too much for my short legs by then. After all, we have to walk back, too." Secretly, Emily had wanted to show Hank she could keep up with him, but she wasn't sure she could do it. They'd already walked several blocks to get to the bridge. The bridge center would be a logical goal for her, too.

Boys on roller skates passed them, and curious to identify sounds coming up behind, they turned. A tap dancer closed the gap between them. He was tapping his way forward with what seemed endless energy and determination.

"San Francisco's gone crazy!" said Emily. "Hank wants to see the ceremonies at Crissy Field. They'll have floats and marching bands, trick riders, pipers, and even a Wells Fargo stagecoach. But after this circus, I don't know if I want to leave and miss it. Who could top what's going on here?"

"I bet I can," Hank said abruptly.

Alert, the group expected to see him point out another stunt. Instead, he took Emily's hand and drew her aside. Her family hung back for a moment then edged forward slowly. Emily looked into Hank's mesmerizing eyes.

"What, Hank?" she whispered, afraid her dream wouldn't come true.

Hank knelt on one knee. "Emily Anderson, I love you more than I thought I could love anyone. Will you marry me? Please?"

It had happened. On the Golden Gate Bridge, May 27, 1937, with a ship passing below and three airplanes flying overhead, Hank had asked her to marry him, and God had led her all the way. Tears filled Emily's eyes. "Hank Garrett, I love you the same way, and yes, I will marry you."

Hank got up, took her in his arms, and while the others waited to hug them, they kissed for a long, ecstatic moment.

Suddenly, a man shouted. "Listen! Stop! Listen!"

In an instant the crowd around them quieted. Above them, the wind, the wires, the cables, and the tower combined to play an unimaginable symphony. Organ-like bass tones resonated upward, yielding scales of higher tones, and as the wind changed, the sounds went on, full and free. For that moment in history, the bridge was singing its own praises, telling all who heard that it existed and that it would enrich the world.

"Such a sound," Hank murmured, holding Emily close. "On the day you became mine. Thank You, Lord."

fifteen

"Well, Son, I didn't expect to see you! Are you going to be with us overnight?" said Mr. Garrett, closing the front door and hanging his son's hat in the foyer closet.

"Yes, but I have to get back to San Francisco tomorrow. I just had an errand down here." He grinned slightly.

The two men talked as they wandered to the parlor off a wide paneled hallway. Smiling, Hank's mother, reclining on a lounge with soft pillows at her back, raised her plump face for his kiss on her cheek. Her robe was heavy chenille, and on her feet were woolen socks. That meant her arthritis was bad today. Sitting forward in her armchair, Frances closed her magazine and placed it in the magazine rack at her side. When Hank kissed her cheek, too, tears moistened her eyes.

"Your girlfriend thoroughly impressed the folks on their visit to San Francisco. I'm eager to meet her," she said.

"We're eager to see her again, too, but I'm just as glad she didn't come this time." His mother's usually neat gray hair was uncombed, carelessness that was further proof of her pain.

Hank pretended not to notice. "She's occupied with her brother's wedding plans. In fact, I have things to talk about regarding Clay and Celia. That's one reason I'm here."

"Are we invited to their wedding?" asked Mr. Garrett. "I'd be disappointed if we weren't."

"Shall we be seated?" Hank said. "This is a special trip for me. I came to tell you something I doubt will be a surprise."

Mr. Garrett smiled and sat with Hank on a couch, and the two women made themselves comfortable as they waited for Hank to speak.

"Father, I told you I'd be using some of my money right away, and I have. Clay has his own garage now. He's a hard worker and has all the business he can handle. It's money invested in a happy future."

"He's a good boy. After the way the family's treated you, I'd say you did the right thing," said Mr. Garrett. "I'd have helped if I'd known sooner that Clay was so discouraged."

Hank smiled at his father's new attitude. Since Hank had been saved, his relationship with his family had changed. Not only did they respect him, he respected them. They had all made mistakes, but he realized he should have tried harder to get along. Quarrels solved nothing; Christ had a better way.

"Clay and Celia will be all right now," he said. "Their plans are to have the wedding at Celia's home."

"Inside or out?" asked Mrs. Garrett.

"It's a garden wedding." Hank crossed his stretched-out legs and looked up at the ceiling. "The real reason I came is to tell you I've asked Emily to marry me." He grinned and looked from one to the other.

After a moment's hesitation, his parents happily vocalized their approval. Frances stood back until they were calm again, then she congratulated Hank with a hug.

"She must be pretty special to win Mother and Father over so completely. I'm glad for you, Hank. Really."

But Hank sensed the melancholy in her tone and rushed to spring a surprise. "Frances, when she and I marry, Emily wants you to be part of it. She's also got a bee in her bonnet about someone she'd like you to meet. Their administrator. He's a Christian, but she thinks you'd like him. I do, too, so keep an open mind while you're in San Francisco. I guarantee, you won't have the heart to refuse her," he said with confidence.

Flushing a nice shade of pink, Frances sent him a smile.

Hank's father cleared his throat. "So when is Clay's wedding taking place, Son?"

❧

"Hank! You're back!" Clay threw open the door to let him in. "Hope your folks were in the pink. Hey, Em, your knight in shining armor is here," he called, grinning at their visitor.

"Be right there," called Emily from the kitchen. "Celia and I are bringing lemonade."

Hank laughed. "Where's *your* shining armor, sport?"

"Won her without it, Hank. She's an angel," Clay declared as Hank looked around the cozy living room and took a seat.

The Anderson home had taken on a charm that the two talented women had created with needles and thread. Curtains, slipcovers, and pillows brightened this and every other room. He had also seen bargain pieces of furniture, from secondhand stores and household sales, refinished to new life at their skilled hands. Discreetly elegant Americana, it was the kind of home he wanted.

"You're a fortunate man, Clay. So am I."

Flicking a glance at the dining room door, Clay raised his voice. "Well, I was pretty sure someone would take Emily off our hands sooner or later, but it's too bad a nice guy like you got stuck with her."

Emily rounded the door, her hands like claws and her red fingernails bared. "Talk behind my back, will you? Let me at him!"

Clay cowered and covered his head with his arms. "Help, help! Get this madwoman off me!"

Hank stood, chuckling. "Sorry, pal. You got into this one by yourself. Besides," he murmured in an intimate voice, "she doesn't look too fierce to me."

Emily turned and went into his arms for a brief kiss. "Now *that's* the way to handle a woman, Clay. You'll have to get Hank to teach you."

Carrying the lemonade tray, Celia set it on a table next to Clay's chair. "Let's sit close," she said and dragged a padded stool toward Clay. "We have a proposal for you."

Sitting beside Hank with his arm around her shoulders, Emily drew a deep breath. "We're ready. What's on your minds?"

"We propose having a double wedding!" said Clay.

Emily and Hank exchanged a look—Emily surprised, and Hank perplexed.

"Are you sure?" Emily said, glancing at Hank and reaching for his hand.

The house was quiet. Stanley, Sarah, and Tim had gone to bed. Hank hoped Emily would speak first.

"If you'll consent, we'd love to make it a double wedding," said Celia.

Emily was waiting for him. "What do your folks think about doubling the guest list?" said Hank.

"It will take a little more planning, that's all. But it can be done. I can think of one answer now—we borrow tables and chairs from the church. Except for the trellis we'll use as an altar, so many flowers are in bloom there's no need for more decorations. We'll add more ribbons if we need them."

"Our parents will help, of course," Emily said.

"Sure, they will," said Clay. "The main thing is, we should be married together. What do you think?"

Hank knew Emily sensed his tension. She was wondering if he was considering a double wedding only to please her. In the next second, she verified it.

"Hank," she said, "I'm not sure you want this. I believe before we decide, we should be frank and say what's on our minds. Tell us what *you* think."

"All right, I will. But it's going to be a shock. Can you take it? Seems like I'm always pulling surprises on you." His eyes probed those of the other three. They were waiting. "All right, here goes. I'm rich. I don't mean just rich. I'm filthy rich, as they say."

Three dismayed people stared without speaking. Then, the glow of insight swept Clay's face.

"*You're* the one. . . ."

Hank held up his hand. "Let me explain. To prove to myself I could make my own fortune, I refused to use money from my grandfather, held in trust for me. Big money didn't matter to you and your family, Emily, because you had God's concept of values. When I became a Christian, I grasped that concept, too.

"The money began to bother me because my refusal of it had caused a rift between my parents and me. For the first time, when I was in Los Angeles, after I found the Lord, I wanted to be reconciled with them. It happened, and that's why they came to San Francisco. We've developed a good relationship, and we talk often on the phone now. The reason I'm telling you is because you'd have to know about the money sooner or later, and this seems the ideal time."

"Hank," said Emily, her eyes wide and luminous, "what

are you saying? Does this mean we'll live a different kind of life? I'm not a social butterfly, you know."

Hank hugged her. "Praise the Lord!" He felt her relax against him. "We'll live just as we're living now, except we'll have homes of our own. Hasn't anyone thought of that but me? We'll have children to raise in Christ's name, and we'll be doing great things for the Lord. . .together!"

The other three smiled as they individually pondered his words.

"Now. About the wedding. My folks would like very much to stage a double wedding for us at the Fairmont Hotel ballroom. They would also like to cater the reception. We'll make it the most beautiful wedding in the world if you'll say the word."

Emily and Celia were without utterance.

Shocked, Clay tried. "I thought rich people were. . . Hey, Hank, are you telling the truth? You're a regular guy."

"Yes, I'm telling the truth." Hank's serious tone continued. "Listen to me, and believe me. If you would do us this favor, it would give my parents a chance to be in my life as they haven't been for too many years. Won't you let them? It's up to you, but please, let's do it, okay?"

Emily found breath to answer. "Hank, Celia and I haven't dresses for the Fairmont Hotel."

"If you two say yes, everything will be taken care of. You can still use the dresses you've made after we're married. But for our weddings, please, let us attire you in the height of fashion. Be fairy princesses, and do this for *me*, Emily. Celia? Please?"

Emily's head fell back against the sofa. "Is this really happening?"

"I don't know, Emily," Celia gasped. "My head's spinning."

Clay laughed. "Can't be my fault—I haven't kissed you for an hour."

Rolling her eyes, Emily said seriously, "The thing that bothers me is how it will affect your parents, Celia. Won't they be disappointed after all their work?"

"I can't imagine their being disappointed that I would be married in the Fairmont Hotel ballroom!" Celia said breathlessly. "Do your parents really want to do this, Hank?"

"Yes. I went down to tell them Emily and I were getting married, and they came up with the whole plan. Your parents will get a letter from them today or tomorrow, and I'll talk to Emily's folks myself. But first, I needed this private moment to find out if it was all right with the three of you." Hank cuddled Emily against his shoulder. "Well, how about it? Will you consent?"

❧

"Oh, Emily, you look just beautiful!" Celia cried.

She touched the diaphanous veil flowing from Emily's Juliet cap and encircling her wedding gown of gossamer lace.

"What about you? Did you ever dream we'd have two such stunning gowns for our wedding? The princess style is just right for you. It gives you a regal look, and so does that chic crown for your veil. Celia, if I'm dreaming, don't wake me!"

A tall slender lady with short chestnut hair and a clipboard in her hand came into the fitting room. "If you young ladies are ready," said the wedding counselor, "our models are dressed in some of the going-away costumes you'll need to complete your ensembles."

She turned to her assistant, "Let's get them out of these wedding gowns and into robes so they can go out to the showroom." She turned to the brides. "Your mothers are having tea and are eagerly waiting to know if this is the final fitting on the gowns. I'm happy to say it is."

"I don't think mine could fit any better. Could yours, Celia?" Emily said, enraptured with her reflection in the mirror.

"Not in a million years!" cooed Celia.

"Then we're happy to have been of service to the Andersons and the Grants." The counselor added a note to the clipboard. "Now, you will be posed by our newspaper photographer two days before the wedding, so the pictures will come out on the day after the wedding. The Garretts are sending a photographer from Los Angeles, too."

She smiled her department store smile. "My dears, this is such an exciting time for our store. Even in San Francisco, it's rare to have a double wedding with two such beautiful brides!"

⁂

Frances, whom Emily had come to know well in the last month, had capably supported her as maid of honor. She had broken down, surprising Emily with tearful sentiment at losing her brother to the married state. Instantly, Emily saw a wedding for her new sister-in-law as an absolute necessity; she and Celia simply had to find the right man.

Emily was glad Celia had chosen Loretta to be her matron of honor. She meant a lot to Emily, too. Loretta had hired her to teach at Ocean Gardens Christian School.

"Thank goodness she's already married, Emily," Celia joked. "Talented as we are, I don't think we could possibly come up with *two* eligible bachelors!"

Since he would be her pastor from that day on, Celia and her family agreed that the Andersons' pastor should officiate.

Attendants for their wedding were selected friends.

Now, the big day was here.

Although the styles of the girls' gowns were different, their faces, above the white roses of their bouquets, shone alike with happiness.

On the arms of their fathers, Emily and Celia made their entrance before two diagonal aisles between the seated guests. Passing their families and dozens of friends, they moved toward a flower-banked altar where Hank and Clay waited, dressed in cutaway coats and striped trousers.

When Celia and Clay said their vows, tears sprang to Emily's eyes for the first time, and she knew what Frances was feeling. But Emily's were happy tears. Celia knew the Lord and had been her sister of the heart since the day they met. Frances needed to come to the Savior. She would; Emily knew she would. Then she would know the abundant life Hank had received.

Please, Lord, let it happen, Emily prayed. *And give Clay and Celia a life in You that will shine on those around them for as long as they live.*

The pastor then addressed Emily and Hank. As Hank slipped her wedding ring on her finger, Emily prayed, *Dear God, let our marriage begin a lifetime in You, no matter what comes. Help us love each other forever as we do now.*

Their minister raised his voice with a smile. "I now pronounce you men and wives. You may kiss your brides."

Hank looked deep into Emily's eyes. As his lips lowered to hers, she rejoiced in the reality that she was his wife. Her dream had come true. Their Savior had brought into being the union He had planned from the beginning.

A Letter To Our Readers

Dear Reader:

In order that we might better contribute to your reading enjoyment, we would appreciate your taking a few minutes to respond to the following questions. We welcome your comments and read each form and letter we receive. When completed, please return to the following:

Rebecca Germany, Fiction Editor
Heartsong Presents
PO Box 719
Uhrichsville, Ohio 44683

1. Did you enjoy reading *At the Golden Gate?*
    ☐ Very much. I would like to see more books by this author!
    ☐ Moderately
    I would have enjoyed it more if _____

    _____

    _____

2. Are you a member of **Heartsong Presents**? Yes ☐ No ☐
    If no, where did you purchase this book? _____

    _____

3. How would you rate, on a scale from 1 (poor) to 5 (superior), the cover design? _____

4. On a scale from 1 (poor) to 10 (superior), please rate the following elements.

    _____ Heroine   _____ Plot

    _____ Hero   _____ Inspirational theme

    _____ Setting   _____ Secondary characters

5. These characters were special because_____
   _____
   _____

6. How has this book inspired your life?_____
   _____
   _____

7. What settings would you like to see covered in future
   Heartsong Presents books?_____
   _____
   _____

8. What are some inspirational themes you would like to see
   treated in future books?_____
   _____
   _____

9. Would you be interested in reading other **Heartsong
   Presents** titles?   Yes ☐   No ☐

10. Please check your age range:
    ☐ Under 18   ☐ 18-24   ☐ 25-34
    ☐ 35-45   ☐ 46-55   ☐ Over 55

11. How many hours per week do you read?_____

Name _____

Occupation _____

Address _____

City _____ State _____ Zip _____

British Columbia

The early twentieth century not only births the town of Dawson Creek, British Columbia, but changes it from a prairie village into the southern anchor of the Alcan Highway. Follow the fictionalized growth of author Janelle Burnham Schneider's hometown through the eyes of characters who hold onto hopes, dreams. . .and love.

This captivating volume combines four complete novels of inspiring love that you'll treasure.

paperback, 464 pages, 5 ³⁄₁₆" x 8"

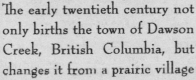

Hearts♥ng Presents
Love Stories
Are Rated G!

That's for godly, gratifying, and of course, great! If you love a thrilling love story, but don't appreciate the sordidness of some popular paperback romances, **Heartsong Presents** is for you. In fact, **Heartsong Presents** is the *only inspirational romance book club* featuring love stories where Christian faith is the primary ingredient in a marriage relationship.

Sign up today to receive your first set of four, never before published Christian romances. Send no money now; you will receive a bill with the first shipment. You may cancel at any time without obligation, and if you aren't completely satisfied with any selection, you may return the books for an immediate refund!

Imagine. . .four new romances every four weeks—two historical, two contemporary—with men and women like you who long to meet the one God has chosen as the love of their lives. . . all for the low price of $9.97 postpaid.

To join, simply complete the coupon below and mail to the address provided. **Heartsong Presents** romances are rated G for another reason: They'll arrive *Godspeed!*